MISS FULLER

MISS FULLER

A Novel

❧

APRIL BERNARD

STEERFORTH PRESS
HANOVER, NEW HAMPSHIRE

For information about permission to reproduce
selections from this book, write to:
Steerforth Press L.L.C., 45 Lyme Road, Suite 208,
Hanover, New Hampshire 03755

Library of Congress Cataloging-in-Publication Data

Bernard, April.
 Miss Fuller / April Bernard. -- 1st ed.
   p. cm.
 ISBN 978-1-58642-195-3 (alk. paper)
 1. Fuller, Margaret, 1810-1850--Fiction. 2. Feminists--Fiction. I. Title.
 PS3552.E7258M57 2012
 813'.54--dc23
                        2012003390

Book design by Peter Holm, Sterling Hill Productions

1 3 5 7 9 10 8 6 4 2

for Henry

ONE

News of the wreck made everyone want to be up and going, doing something, talking, moving, to keep the knowledge from puddling and festering. It was a hot July, in the year 1850. Margaret Fuller, their old friend, together with her husband and young son, had been ship-wrecked and drowned, on their voyage home from Europe. No one in the Thoreau house had slept.

"It's Bedlam!" said Mother, as if the sight of Mr. Emerson coming up the path made it official. One went to see Mr. Emerson; he did not pay calls himself, and certainly not before breakfast. He dipped his massive head slightly as he came through the door, a Colossus visiting the Pygmies. Mother's nose came up about even with his middle waist-coat button.

Mr. Emerson had come to ask Henry to go from Concord to New York and then Fire Island, the site of the wreck, to claim the bodies and other remains. With luck, yet how ridiculous to speak as if luck could ever again be hoped for, Henry would find her book manuscript.

Anne, his youngest sister, helped Henry pack his satchel. She always helped him if he let her. She tried to persuade him that as this was a delicate errand he would need her to accompany him.

"The ocean may well have stripped her clothes," she said.

He said, "A dead woman is like any dead animal."

———

It had been nearly a decade earlier, when Anne was twelve years old, that she had first, as she said, "encountered" Miss Fuller. She and her oldest sister, Helen, sometimes still called one of the "girls" although she was well into her twenties, had traveled as guests of Mrs. Deaver on a special trip into Boston. Trips to Boston were the height of excitement, but Anne was always ready to go anywhere, even the next town. All other destinations were known to be inferior to Boston — including New York, Washington, and London — with the possible exception of Concord itself and the home of a distinguished relative, a judge, who lived on a promontory in Marblehead. Anne, adopted and by far the youngest in the family, looked forward to Marblehead — someday, they said, she would see it — with especial awe.

Meanwhile, there were the reliable glories of Boston. The always fashionable Mrs. Deaver had purchased a subscription to something called "Conversations," which title she pronounced with a self-conscious slowing and mouthing, as if the syllables were Italian: *"Con-verr-sass-ee-on-es."* Mrs. Deaver had taken a European tour.

For some time Miss Fuller had been "offering" Conversations, on topics of "general interest to ladies of culture," usually at the Peabody home in West Street. But for this exceptional occasion, raising funds for a new progressive school, it was to be a larger gathering at the grander home of Mrs. Vaughn. There had been some confusion and embarrassment about whether or not the girls would need to purchase tickets, but Mrs. Deaver convinced their mother she was welcome to bring them along as guests. Anne was deemed just old enough to behave herself; Sissy, the middle sister, was nursing a slight cough, and had decided to stay at home. The cough may have been a convenience, as she was inclined to regard such outings as frivolous. Helen was perfectly polite but they were to know that she condescended by accepting the invitation. Their brothers John and Henry, meanwhile, had made the breakfast table raucous with predictable jokes about the dangers of the Thoreau girls "conversing."

"John 'converses' nineteen to the dozen," said Helen crossly from her corner of the stagecoach, "and Henry in *certain moods* would talk over the last trumpet."

The railroad lines commencing to cross-hatch New England had not reached Concord quite yet in 1841. So it was the Boston stagecoach, on that day offering the unexpected luxury of no other passengers, that shielded them from the March sleet, as they were tucked up with blankets and hot bricks wrapped in burlap to warm their feet. Anne reached down to feel the heat from the bricks through her gloves.

Mrs. Deaver inquired politely about their brothers' school and Helen fibbed, saying that attendance was still growing, and they had great hopes for the summer term. There were no such hopes; the school was not making enough to pay and their brothers were exhausted by the work. Anne gamely seconded her sister's remarks, as she often did, with a quiet, "Indeed." This old-womanish habit she had picked up from one of her mother's friends. When Anne needed to disagree, she applied equal economy of means. "Do you really think so," without the interrogative lift, expressed a quiet nay without committing her to the labor and peril of voicing a counter-argument. Her family, who would have liked the argument much better, found this tiresome. No doubt that was the chief reason she persisted.

Mrs. Deaver proceeded to "sell" them on their forthcoming treat.

"The first time I went, in December, it was most elevating. The Peabody ladies have a little shop, completely refined, with hundreds of books and pamphlets. We met in the 'book room,' very cozy. I tried to just get the feeling of the thing, not as a participant of the *Conversatione* myself, just a learner, a student. Well, not knowing anything certainly did not restrain Mrs. Delapont; nor her cousin from New York.

She opened all of her remarks with 'In New York,' so as we'd know. 'In New York, the question of archaic architecture in private homes, especially broken columns *à la grecque*, is quite settled.' In New York!"

Helen smiled at Anne.

"No one cared, it was entirely a different matter from what Miss Fuller was offering for our consideration, which I believe concerned the large spaces of a geometrically pleasing kind, as in the ancient Acropolis, which is built on the Golden Mean. Things in proportion, 'the assistance they offer for thought.'"

"Some people," said Helen, "have been known to think perfectly well in meditation cells. Or prisons."

"Certainly, yes, but would they not have thought better and more, more *widely*, on the Acropolis? That's just the sort of conversation one can run with, as it were, with Miss Fuller in the room. She's got the force of large ideas, even if I'm not sure where the ideas lead because I don't have the reading. Such vistas — Greek, which I believe Miss Fuller actually reads, and those heathen classical stories which are really so wise and not at all in contradiction to our own Bible if read rightly, as — *allegories*."

"Miss Fuller is, I believe, excessively educated?"

"Dear me yes, her father trained her as if she had been a boy. It's made her goggle-eyed and very odd, of course, but she is a female genius, certainly, though I can't say if I know that she is a model of the New Woman, as Elizabeth

Peabody claims, or something simply unique —. She speaks like a wonder, can quote anything at all."

"I trust that the slavery question will be addressed."

"Not this afternoon — more classics, I think. She does know so many languages. Greek, as I said, Latin, Italian, French, German, and I think someone said she was studying Hebrew, which seems peculiar."

"Henry says that we should all study American," said Anne.

Mrs. Deaver barked a laughing "Hah!"

"Henry is *our* genius, especially Anne's," said Helen.

"How droll," said Mrs. Deaver. The girls should not worry about their dresses, she went on, as no one would expect them to measure up to Boston fashion. Country girls, she elaborated, might even be said to be in bad taste should they attempt to dress like city girls. She said that skirts were even wider than last winter and that the very latest thing was cuffs decorated with colored silk fancy-work sheathed in Bruges lace.

Anne fingered her plain cuffs of dark red merino, the same fabric and color as the rest of her best coat and dress. Helen, in dark blue, moved her head in a way that could not quite be called "tossing" and looked out the window, apparently seized by a sudden interest in melting snow.

"Surely," she said, staring out, "we should prefer quality and enduring modest beauty of dress to fashionable fripperies."

As Mrs. Deaver adjusted her shoulder cape, revealing her own splendidly embroidered and lace-covered dress cuffs, she demurred, slightly: "I was not speaking of fandoodles and bric-a-brac, dear. Certainly nothing like those turban tassels on Angela Sawyer's aunt when she visited in the fall."

The memory of the tassels, and the head that had so unwisely worn them, allowed them all to share in the delight of a shocked pause. Helen arranged herself and embarked on a summary of Mr. Garrison's most recent editorial in the *Liberator*, which editorial both of her listeners had in point of fact already read. Although she accepted a chicken wing from the hamper, she did not pause to take a bite until they passed the Common, when she at last took account of the food she had been using as a sort of conductor's stick.

The Vaughn house occupied most of an entire block; Anne discarded her first impressions that it was a municipal hall or a theatre, and took in the fact that it was an actual residence. Mrs. Deaver looked suddenly, ludicrously, shy, as if the granite of her face were visibly eroding to shale and about to slide away. At least the sleet had stopped; the street and steps were dry. Helen tugged at her gloves with an air. If she could gird up, then so could Anne; she retied her bonnet, patted her coil of braids at the back, and gripped the iron railing of the front steps.

Of the preliminaries Anne remembered little, for like an animal in peril she concentrated almost entirely on danger from the moment she stepped inside. Relieved of coat and bonnet, she shrank back, ducking her head to shield her eyes against the brilliance of the reception hall. Helen, graceful and pretty and lit up by the company, led the way as always, greeting and being introduced. Anne stayed at her sister's side *like an ape on a leash*, she thought.

Glimpsing her face in one of the large gilt-framed looking-glasses was a help. She would not, at any rate, hop or gibber. Her face, arguing with her own metaphor, was not at all simian, not like Henry's and Sissy's. The Thoreau chin was a family trouble, and Sissy's was the worst of all, with that bulge as if she held a whole potato in her mouth. Henry and their father had the chin as well, but were saved by sidewhiskers as effective disguise, or rather, counter-balance. Mother, Helen, and John were the handsome ones.

Anne, whose only knowledge of her own ancestry was that she was Mother's third cousin and had been born in Maine, was just different: tall for her age and fair, not especially pretty but clever enough. She suddenly wished she were an actual monkey, like the one a family friend had brought home from the tropics. It died of a cold after a couple of months, but Henry had taken her to visit when it was alive. The monkey's owner had let it out of the cage, and it ran up the book-shelves and sat and chittered on the mantel-shelf over the parlor fire. With its small pink face rimmed in white fur like an Esquimau's, round dark eyes, and shaggy grey body that looped about into a long curled tail, it was as fetching as any play-thing. It had bitten her hand hard enough to draw blood. A nasty beast, but kin.

A monkey in Mrs. Vaughn's bright hall could swing up on the curtains and the lamp fittings and no doubt thoroughly avoid conversation. Would a monkey chew on the furniture? That table looked like a glossy caramel cake. Like floating cake. All the furniture — in the bright hall, in the parlor, in the far dining room — seemed to be floating above the ground. It looked dangerously insubstantial; and indeed when she bumped a table it skidded a distance as she jerked back with a stifled shriek. The chairs and tables were actually fitted with gilt feet, tiny wheeled slippers, as if they were about to dash off to a ball. Someone said the furniture was French.

More danger — in the form of strange faces that looked and then quickly looked away, or worse, looked and stared — manifested itself. And the ladies were, as Mrs. Deaver had forecast, in disconcertingly wide skirts. Upside-down flowers: Several of the younger ladies appeared to have sprouted a corolla of stiff petals opening out from a tiny calyx of waist, which petals drooped to the floor. In this inverted vision, the arms were leaves and the neck, the brief stem. *Viola bostonia* or perhaps *Lupinus peabodacea.* Curls bounced, framing each maiden forehead as so many corkscrewed roots, and the air in the rooms surrounded these delicate roots with a sort of pellucid mulch. Water flowers? *Nymphaea conversationis.* She decided to sketch her visions, once she was safely home with her paper and drawing pencils; she barely heard the questions posed about her family, her interest in antiquity, and the depth of Concord snows. Her drawing began to take shape in her mind — it was of lady-flowers in a glass vase and a monkey, fingering their skirts, arrayed upon a table-top that resembled a sugar-iced cake.

Two ladies wearing spectacles were introduced, their eyes nearly invisible as the lenses flashed with reflected light. One was the elder Miss Peabody, Elizabeth, the teacher and editor, who immediately turned away to begin speaking to someone else; the other was her sister Mary. Mary told Anne that she had heard of her interest in art. When she lowered her head confidentially, her eyes were revealed, wet and golden-brown as a trout's.

"At present," said Mary, "my sister Sophia — she is not here today but is home with a *migraine* — has been engaged to copy the Copley portrait in Mrs. Vaughn's sitting room. If it is a success, Mrs. Vaughn will hang it in her summer house."

"I also have a sister Sophia — we always call her Sissy — who is also at home, with a chill. But she does not paint — and I have never taken lessons."

"With our two *Sophias* absent, we must count on Miss Fuller to make up the deficit of *wisdom*."

The Peabody sisters were jostled away before any more could be said. In later years Anne would remember Mary's lugubrious remark as a kind of emblem of the heavy, un-amused repartee known as "Boston wit."

Now the movement of the crowd was prodigious; perhaps the ladies as well as the chairs had little gilt wheels on their feet; certainly they moved in a gliding motion, when given ample width of floor to cross, their skirts swaying in a synco-pated rhythm, a half beat behind each forward plunge, like the skirts of skaters. It was almost impossible to tell about the feet by looking; as well as fashionably wider, the Boston ladies' skirts were also markedly longer. Helen, although like Anne limp of skirt and exposed of ankle, was charm-ing a pair of elderly ladies she had just met — they clasped her between them as they all sashayed — by scolding them about slavery in Texas.

A largish woman in shiny magenta silk blocked half the entrance to the large room set up for the Conversation. This must be Miss Fuller — her calyx-waist was not small, her large bust was not fully subdued by her corsets, and the sense of something barely pinned down, like a tent in a gale, was present in the bulges of her figure, the large fair hair fixed it appeared in many places but still sliding to one side, the curls jigging at her temples, and in the movement of her arms, which seemed to be gesturing in great labor against an invisible wind. Helen tugged on her sister's hand and they made their way to a settee beside Mrs. Deaver, who had found a chair and was trying and only just failing to look regal.

Tiny Mrs. Vaughn smiled as everyone sat down and then amidst approving chuckles found a footstool on which to stand. She spoke a few words of appreciation for the pleasure — or perhaps she should say, the pleasurable effort of the mind — they were about to share with Miss Fuller. Her erudition, her writing for and editing of *The Dial*, and the fascinating pamphlet newly published about the education of young ladies — copies are available in the reception room and of course at the Misses Peabodys' shop, yes, those lovely blue covers, and at a nominal cost for Conversation subscribers to defray publication expenses only — were familiar to them all, she hoped. Yes, the proceeds from today's special talk would be for Mrs. Somebody Mumble's new school — modeled with the guidance of Mr. Horace Mann — and we are all enthusiasts for the progressive education of young women. Naturally, as this is a theme of Miss Fuller's talks, and of her life, she has generously agreed to speak on behalf of this cause.

("Does she receive a fee today then?" Anne whispered. Helen almost imperceptibly shrugged.)

Today — and the ladies were urged to take care, as teacups were now being passed amongst them, and yes that is Mrs. Wadsworth's famous marmalade sponge! — they would be taking up the thread dropped with such suspense before in December: What Can the Classical Age Teach Us About Woman Today?

Anne spilt her tea entirely out of her cup and smeared jam

on her sleeve. In the midst of her shame, which mounted as Miss Fuller's advance to the front of the room was delayed by the mopping and dabbing of several napkins, she closed her eyes and subsided into a stunned stillness. For some time she was not able to listen. Eventually the French-horn notes of Miss Fuller's most emphasized words came through, as the mortified pulse of blood in her head beat less fiercely to the speaker's rhythm:

". . . Not so much the *Greeks* as the *Romans* . . . *Education* . . . *Reverence* for the *Female Principle*, which we must not confuse with reverence for the *Actual Females*, the *Wives* and *Daughters*. But there were *Rights* of *Woman* as well as *Man*, in corners of that empire and in many other societies . . ."

Gradually Anne came to understand that no one was looking at her. It was just a cup of tea, nothing even broken, and if the stain persisted they could turn the sleeve at home. No one was looking at her.

Miss Fuller now was clearly speaking about the present day, and Anne opened her eyes to wonder how they had vaulted over the centuries so quickly. Helen beside her was at full attention — the subject was the need today, in Boston and throughout this country, to explore the full capacities of both men and women.

"You ask, But will not women cease to be womanly, if they are thrust into the spheres of learning, of philosophy, of political life? I do not urge any 'thrusting,' no such unnatural movement, but only what is natural, the leaning towards, through inclinations which are as in-born in some women as they are in most men. Certainly most women must continue to be womanly, and concerned with children, with home and hearth, with all the fine things that make our lives noble and sweet — producing such matchless sponge and tea as we have drunk — and spilt — here today. . . ." Miss Fuller paused.

Laughter fluttered through the room. They were looking at her again. Some more moments passed; life returned.

". . . For how many of us may be destined for a public stage? Not from eagerness to perform for applause, but from a sense of duty, of the rightness of a crusade? If we do not change our minds about what women may do, how can we hope to change the injustice, the poverty, and the mistreatment of fellow souls whom we see daily about us? If we cannot change our minds about what women may do, how can we, my sisters, hope to see the world change for the better and make its progress to that Finer Day we await in our hearts and minds and souls?"

A brocade drapery, of silvery blue, swagged the window recess behind Miss Fuller. It looked like a ship's sail. Anne began counting the panes in the enormous windows.

"Surely you have yourselves known someone — an aunt, a mother, a sister, or you, your own self — who has an *inclination* towards some area of thought or action that our prejudices say cannot, or should not, be entertained? How often have I heard that a young woman should not be taught Greek, as it will damage her brain, stunt her growth, possibly unfit her for life itself — and yet how I loved to learn Greek, and Latin, and the mathematics, and to read philosophy. And I dare say, these years later, that I am healthy enough."

Each window was three rows high, each row of four tall panes each, with an arch at the top, of glass panels in a fan pattern. The windows looked on a desolate wintry back garden; as Anne craned her neck to watch, a white terrier with brown spots sped down a path.

"Has any young girl of your acquaintance a knack for the natural sciences? Can you imagine a day when she might study the sciences at a college, as men do? We have heard of such colleges, small ones, established in Switzerland and in France so that women may gaze through telescopes and explore the bituminous horizons of chemistry, just within these last few years. Think of Miss Herschel, England's famed Comet Catcher! Why not here? Why should the world of science, the glorious future of our understanding, be deprived of those intellects which are suited for her study and promulgation?

"Some of you may have heard the story about my little adventure — near misadventure — at the Harvard College Library. It is a sanctum forbidden to women; and yet I knew of its heavy-laden shelves, its reference volumes, encylcopediae and records and almanacks from other centuries and other countries. As I was laboring on a translation from the

German last year, I found that I too wished to consult some of these books, and a friend offered to go to the library for me, to consult a reference work, in German, about the reign of Catherine the Great — my problem concerned military matters on the Russian steppe in the last century — but I declined his kind offer. For one thing, his knowledge of German was inferior to my own. For another, I knew myself to be embarked on a work of serious, and valuable, scholarship. I knew also that any man from anywhere in the world engaged in such work would be able to use the Harvard Library. And so —"

Miss Fuller paused for the full effect, her forehead glistening. Anne was still looking into the garden. The terrier had a grey squirrel in his mouth and was shaking it vigorously.

"Yes, I did! I walked right up the steps of the famed Gore Hall. I ignored the initial efforts to impede me, I announced to the librarians the nature of my task, and — I think they were simply too amazed to stop me — I found my books, solved my problem, and, much to the evident dismay of the door-keeper, I have been a faithful visitor to that sanctum ever since!"

She needed to wait for the exclamations, laughter, and light applause to die away.

"Yes, I did enjoy my little triumph. Yet I know it to be small indeed. For consider! Is Woman truly revered in any area of life? I do not speak of your individual domestic arrangements where I trust such ladies as yourselves are treated with the respect, with the reverence, due to you from your admirable husbands. Mr. Harvard College himself may have the good manners briefly to forget his own benighted prejudice about women in his library — as a matter of *politeness*. But his law does not change. And in the eyes of the real Law, the laws of the town and the state and the country? We are nothing."

The animals had disappeared into the shrubbery. If Anne closed one eye, the right-hand window was filled with the black blue-green of a fir-tree that pressed against the house. If she closed the other eye, only half the window was dark, and the rest was white with the light of the clouded sky.

"Stop squinting!" Helen hissed and pinched her, hard, on the hand. Fortunately no one noticed, as Miss Fuller was now speaking at an orator's pitch, her dampened fair curls drooping, elongated nearly to her shoulders.

"You have less, in the eyes of the Law, than a seamstress of a hundred years ago, or Shakespeare's Greasy Joan who 'keel'd the pot'! A peasant woman in medieval England, married as she may well have been, owned the humble property her father left her, and owned the property she held with her husband jointly if he died. Those laws were changed in England (and its colonies) in the eighteenth century and changed again, not for the better, thirty years ago. In an effort to shore up its great estates, to keep financial and political power in the hands of its aristocracy, England *dis*-enfranchised its entire female population!

Primogeniture does not only assure the eldest son inherits; it is also another name for pushing women out of whatever public role, whatever autonomous power, they had enjoyed hitherto. In such an era as this, this nineteenth century of progress and industry and the advance of learning and science, it is a shock, a disgrace, that women virtually have been stripped of their dignity and property rights!"

An agitation on the settee signaled what was about to come from Helen.

"Miss Fuller!" Silence, and a craning of all necks. "What about the black men, our brothers in chains, who have no property rights, and not even the rights to their own bodies, and the bodies of their wives and children?"

The speaker reached her hands in a sudden gesture over the heads of her audience, as if she could clasp Helen's. "My dear — You speak for us all — I think I recognize you from the Anti-Slavery Women of Boston —"

"Concord."

"Ah, my beloved Concord, home also to our dear teacher, the great Mr. Emerson. I will tell you, all bold women of Concord and Boston, all lovers of freedom, about the slavery of the Africans and the slavery of all women today — Hush!" She put a finger in the air to stop Helen's next words, and like a silenced child Helen sank back.

"For how can we free the African if we cannot free ourselves? And consider as well our Negro sisters —" This was going a little far, as the sudden intake of breath hissed through the room. "Yes, I say sisters as in God's eyes we are all brothers and sisters, and if the African man is our brother, so surely the African woman is our sister.

"All depend on our strength, all depend on our action — such as we have already seen, in the anti-slavery committees that have been formed. And when I see the great Abolitionist Miss Sarah Grimke speak, I say — Here is a new woman! She can speak from a pulpit, at the lyceum, in the back of a horse-cart, about the rights of man, and surely I, inspired by her example, can also speak about the rights of women!

"Now think again of our Roman ancestors, and think of their intuitive, their glorious religion — but a precursor to Christian light, yet capable of shedding much light of its own. Philosophy and literature often return to the stories of these gods and goddesses, these nymphs and heroes, not because they are quaint and foolish stories — no! Because, as with all sincere religions, they held within them certain seeds of truth.

"Consider Minerva — Goddess of Wisdom, daughter of Jove. In antiquity she is often paired with an owl, the symbol of wisdom.

"Minerva represents the woman's own wisdom, the 'masculine' side of the feminine, if you will, without which we would all be as silly as chicks newly hatched. No doubt some of you have daughters about whom you wonder, Is she but a silly chick? . . . Are any of them here? Yes?"

A certain amount of tittering filled the room. Miss Fuller opened her eyes especially wide and landed on a dowager with an elegantly turned-out young woman next to her.

"Oh, madam, I hope you do not wonder about her — She looks as pretty as anything, but I dare say there is wisdom as well. . . ."

The young woman threw her hands before her face and gasped with embarrassed delight.

"And as we need to exercise our wisdom, so do men today need to exercise their nurturance! Why should men not also be allowed to follow their own — if you will — feminine inclinations? I refer to the kindness of the benevolent father, the spiritual softness of the good preacher, the care that the best schoolmaster will take when instructing his charges.

"Perhaps in other ages, in other climes, we would not have such need of our Minerva goddess to guide us, our own Instructress who carries a wise owl on her shoulder. But today — ladies — we must solicit her to come to us as a dear friend, to guide us. We need leadership, courage, invention from the women of today! How much you can see if you look about you!"

Accepting her applause, Miss Fuller remained for some moments with her arms stretched wide. Then, with an eager look about her, she asked for questions. Some of the ladies wanted to hear more about Minerva. One had recently visited the Temple of Minerva in Rome, and with effort a few details about its appearance were extracted from her — not so large, the building, as expected — dark inside — the guide not a bit helpful — an owl, or was it a pelican? above the door, she thought — no nose on her, on the Minerva, at all.

Helen made one final effort, pointing out that the Romans owned slaves, so were they to be regarded as offering a beacon of freedom from the past in that respect?

"Ah, my learned friend!" said Miss Fuller. "All societies have their weaknesses. But when we consider that the Roman enslavement of their Greek captives was primarily to employ them as tutors in the house-hold, the picture of slavery is very different from what we suffer here."

"That's not entirely correct," began Helen, but, foolish thing, she was standing in the way of a more robust and better-trained horse than she, and got trampled into the dust quite firmly:

"We shall not here quibble about historical detail — we shall save that for another time! And ladies all, may I remind you that with Mr. Wilberforce's heroic leadership in the English Parliament for many years, in the end of the slave trade and the freeing of the slaves in their West Indies Colonies, we have reason to rejoice and be hopeful about the future of ending slavery here as well!"

Some applause, as the ladies congratulated — they knew not what — themselves? Wilberforce? The freed slaves? The West Indies in general?

"And as the sweep of history pushes ahead to freedom, we will endeavor to act so as to make all men, and women, free!"

As the gathering dispersed, Anne walked over to the windows and looked again into the garden. The terrier was jumping and snapping about the base of a small tree where, just above his reach, the squirrel scolded and bobbed on a branch. The squirrel seemed to have lost its tail, but was otherwise quite alive.

They were still tingling on their ride home in the dark. This time a couple from Fitchburg shared the stagecoach with them. Upon learning of the cause of their companions' excitement, the woman remarked that she couldn't abide public speaking, especially from a female, and closed her eyes. Her husband also pretended to sleep.

Mrs. Deaver was delighted at having shown Miss Fuller to her friends, so pleased that the Wonder had performed her magic again. "Didn't I tell you, she has large ideas, she gives you a sense of the breadth of life!"

Helen said that she was an actress, and said it with scorn, but even she did not deny the beauty. Anne said that Mother did not approve of pagan goddesses — that Martha and Mary, and perhaps Ruth, certainly Eve, provide metaphors sufficient for daily use.

Helen said, "Mother is old-fashioned about many things, dear. Look how John and Henry cite the classical at all times! We must not be restrictive, even as Christians.

All metaphors that have use may be invoked — it is the essayist's and speaker's prerogative — and just as the devil may quote scripture, so it seems possible that a lover of human freedom, as we must believe Miss Fuller to be, may pick and choose her talismans from the streets of Imperial Rome —"

Unable to resist, Anne interrupted: "You are talking just like her!"

Helen frowned, but then as quickly her brow cleared, and she laughed along with her sister. "My goodness," she said, "you may be right. And why not? I will condescend to learn. But —" She raised her eyebrows comically.

"We may admire the ancient myths, and the truths they tell — in any case, they are from the Greeks, conquerors and slave-holders themselves. The history of humanity is a sorry story — we must learn from it without making up fairy tales about it."

She laughed again, and reached an arm over Anne's shoulder to hug her close. "She did sometimes make me cross as two sticks, but we all agree she is a fine speaker, what Mother would call a 'reg'lar spell-binder!'"

"She is a — Venus! — when she speaks," said Mrs. Deaver. "Although her Minerva will do for a model, as all the goddesses were beauties."

The Fitchburg man opened his eyes, just barely, to take in this extravagance. He crossed his arms, composed his face into a grim smirk, and closed his eyes again.

Helen and Anne were still wondering if Miss Fuller had been paid for the day's event; Mrs. Deaver said that she probably had received something, since as far as she knew the Conversations were the only means Miss Fuller had to support herself, as she had given up school teaching. Feeling somehow as if they were discussing very dark matters, they talked in soft voices, keeping their secrets from the man in the coach, about further economic wonders: Sophia Peabody who was earning money not only from occasional commissioned copies of master-works but also with her painting of decorations on screens and lamp shades — ten dollars for a vellum shade! twelve for a glass globe! — and her sister Elizabeth who was publishing books and selling them in the shop; various governesses and teachers; one widow who worked as an apothecary's assistant for forty dollars a month; and all the young ladies who gave music and drawing and French lessons. Mrs. Deaver told them about a boarding-house she had heard of in Boston especially established for such working ladies.

Closer to home, with the oppressive presence of the Fitchburg passengers gone, the girls agreed that Miss Fuller speaking was a revelation. Then it was that the physiognomy of the speaker overcame its parts: The bulging eyes rounded into perfect shining planets, the large pale brow seemed to pulse with thought, the mouth curled around her words; and it all seemed distinguished, a new kind of beauty, offering insight and solace to her listeners before the high wind in which she perpetually stood should at last blow her clean away, to the next pressing engagement, the next crowd eager for enlightenment.

———

Early on the already hot July morning, Anne drove Henry to the depot in North Acton to catch the south-bound train for New Haven and New York City. Henry was not yet sure how to get to the site of the wreck on Fire Island but imagined he would take a ferry. Arthur Fuller, one of Margaret's brothers, along with another old friend, Ellery Channing, were planning to meet up with Henry there.

Wearing only one petticoat, Anne was dressed for the weather, but poor Henry looked damp already in his flannel-cloth suit. He carried his small leather satchel on his lap. Anne was expected at a neighbor's farm to help with the haying after she had seen her brother off.

The train pulled into the depot, and the passengers disembarked. A loud and disordered family clambered down, leaving a pile of baggage on the platform behind them as they crossed the street to take breakfast at the inn. Henry said, not for the first time, how much he disliked riding on trains. He said that train travel was an insult to his legs.

Laughing, Anne opened his case, fished out his small note-book and pencil, and wrote:

*Jul.23.'50 Riding insults my legs. I fain would
walk to Timbuktoo; yea, and rather lose my legs
in that effort, than lose my self-respect by gallop-
ing astride some locomotive Behemoth, the devil's
own horse, bound for Perdition.*

A wisp of a smile passed over Henry's mouth before
disappearing into his whiskers, but whatever he might have
said was interrupted by a distinct trill. They looked up
to the depot roof and saw nothing; the trill was repeated,
and they realized the sound came from somewhere amidst
the baggage at their feet. A small cage of wood and wire
contained a bird, charcoal black with a brilliant yellow head
— a Canary-bird covered with soot.

Had someone hung the cage out the train window, right
behind the engine? The bird's head was still yellow, no
doubt because it had jammed it beneath a wing. It was now
frantically preening a tail feather, trying to clean off the
black oily coat.

The train would not leave for another few minutes. After
years of rescues — a beaver kit from the jaws of a hunting
dog; birds, rabbits, and chipmunks from the claws of the
cats; a turtle from the rain-barrel; a half-smothered owlet
tangled in cobwebs in the barn — Henry and Anne did
not even need to discuss what they would do. Anne kept
look-out as Henry tucked the cage beneath his jacket and
hurried to the livery stable across the station yard. The boy

gave him a bucket, a jar of slop soap, and a rag. Anne joined him to assist at the bath. The soot was persistent, but with rinsings and lathering, as the Canary-bird struggled and churned in the bucket, most of the black came off, as well as several feathers. As Anne shook out and wiped down the bars Henry got his hand pecked to blood by the quivering bird he returned to its cage. They tossed in some finely cracked corn and filled the tin water tray affixed to the bars. Anne darted back to the wagon, placed the cage just behind the buck-board seat, and covered it with a meal sack to keep the bird quiet.

At a signal toot from the engine, the platform filled again. The family retrieved its trunks — the boy hollering, a very little girl crying, a larger girl shaking the hollering boy, and the mother and father determinedly refusing to look for the disappeared bird.

Anne again said she wished she were going along. Death was the occasion and although death was terrible, she needed to remind herself so as not actually to smile from the giddy pleasure that filled her every time she heard a train, even when she was not a passenger, or now, as the wheels started to roll and she jumped from the engine's gigantic side-sneeze of steam. Then Henry climbed up, waved, stepped away into the car, and the train hooted and jerked itself away from the platform.

Anne climbed up, shook the reins, and set out on the return to Concord. At the haying, she would help cook and serve dinner and carry egg-nog and vinegar-water to the thirsty men. In this weather everyone watched the sky all day, hurrying to get the hay cut and raked into windrows and pitched into the wagons before the thunder-storms came in late afternoon. She thought of the farmers and clucked the horses to a trot. She was whistling "Go tell Aunt Rhoady, the old grey goose is dead," when again she remembered the death of Miss Fuller — Mrs. Ossoli, perhaps she must be called, or absurdly, the Marchesa. Then the feeling came again and the day that had been bright dulled. She felt the horses slow to a walk under the reins that dropped to her lap. She felt, perhaps, more frightened than sad. A wreck was not something you could avoid, unless of course you never went anywhere. There were certain place-names that crowded her mind, and picture-plates from the geography books whose every detail she had memorized: Tahiti, Bombay, Cairo, Copenhagen, Tierra del Fuego. She wanted to go everywhere, by train and sailing-ship, and see the wide world. Which, perhaps for the first time, seemed mortally dangerous.

But there was another feeling that nudged her. Not fear, not sadness, something else. Amongst them all, at the news of the wreck, there had been an unspoken shadowy *satis-faction* — she could name it now, and touch it. It was like a thick rope you could grasp in the dark. It was the feeling that this had "served her right." Not like the other deaths in the last few years — first the horror of their brother John seized with fever and lock-jaw; then the Emersons' little boy taken by fever; then darling sister Helen flickering and sputtering like a candle flame for many months from consumption, and finally snuffed last year. Unimaginable griefs, each one more terrible than the last, the vanished beloved cried out for in the nights. And all had died as they had lived — blameless, blameless.

Miss Fuller, on the other hand. She was not blameless, not at all; this was a death made for wincing, not weeping. It even made you angrier about the other deaths. She had no one to blame but herself. When the toddler will not stop teasing the cat and then the cat scratches, you say to the child, "See? I told you not to, serves you right."

"We told you," she whispered, but then she was not sure — either that they had, actually, told her; or, indeed, that a death in a hurricane could be said to be anybody's fault. Could it be that she, that they all, were secretly pleased Miss Fuller was dead? Sissy and Mother had been pursing their mouths in identical straight lines that might mean disapproval and maybe also the self-satisfaction that comes with disapproval. But not really *pleased* — that wasn't possible. Miss Fuller was Mr. Emerson's pet, and Mrs. E had petted her too, and Henry had always said he admired her. The Hawthornes and Alcotts and Peabodies were her dear friends. Mr. Greeley, the editor of the *New-York Daily Tribune*, called her a heroine. No one could be glad to see a heroine die.

And the husband, in spite of being an Italian, was a human being. As Africans were human, so certainly were Italians. She had never actually met an Italian, though she had met slaves and freedmen. How terrible — and how *provincial*, her new word of scorn — that she had need to remind herself of the humanity of an Italian. They did not know him, how could they condemn him, even if he were perhaps comical, a comical Count. Or was he a Marquis? Possibly a dancing-teacher, as one wag had suggested. And the baby, good mercy, no one could be glad for the death of a baby, even if they had said for months that it might not be — quite right. Anne was unsure if the whispers had meant the baby was sickly or possibly an idiot, or actually born outside of wedlock — before a marriage? Was there no real marriage? It was dizzying to even think of this — since the whisperers also hissed "Marchesa" and "Catholic," and made mouths around the words "Italian marriage" as if they meant something else.

The family had refused to be impressed when Miss Fuller had left for Europe in 1846. All right that she had lived in New York and written for the reformist *Tribune* about the city slums; all right that she had traveled to the Great Lakes and deplored the mistreatment of the resettled Indians on their tawdry "reservation." But Europe? Mother, Helen, and Sissy were very clear on this: It was not the right thing to have done, to have gone to Europe; neither becoming nor patriotic. Her newspaper columns from London, Paris, and Rome; her interviews with Carlyle and George Sand and Mazzini the revolutionary and Mickiewicz the poet; her exhortations to aid the Italian cause and the causes of all the revolutions popping and fizzing, sometimes booming, over Europe — all went largely unread at their table, certainly unstudied. (Henry did read them, Anne knew, but he rarely spoke of them. One of the aunts had been living with them when Miss Fuller was writing from England and France, and the aunt had been an enthusiast, reading passages aloud. There was relief when she left.) Such a writer and talker should be at home, where they needed her, with the Abolitionist cause. Women's rights, on which Miss Fuller had spoken and written so famously, were another distraction, not to be countenanced in the face of the great wrong of slavery that history had placed before the men and women of the United States. In the last weeks before her death, Helen had sat up in her bed-clothes for long enough to preach a gasping sort of sermon about it. Helen had been far angrier with the likes of Miss Fuller than with the plantation owners and their "stooges" in Congress — who, as she and Mother agreed, had not been bred to know better.

Anne had talked privately with Miss Fuller only once, and that was during one of those summers — a year or so after the Conversation Anne attended — when Miss Fuller had been living in Concord, at the Emerson home. In large groups, such as the lemonade parties Mrs. E hosted, Miss

Fuller was expansive, full of opinions, and only fell silent when Mr. E spoke. She made sheep's eyes at Mr. E — everyone saw it, including Mrs. E, though she would never say so. Anne guessed that was one reason Mrs. E was so gracious. Helen commented on Miss Fuller's diminished figure, and Henry reported that she was attempting a "vegetary" regimen, some combination of something called the Graham System and one pressed upon her by friends from London who followed Oriental dietary laws. Mrs. E had been making a great effort to satisfy her guest's appetite, but everyone could see she was looking thin and wan, and Mrs. E felt blamed.

One afternoon Henry took his sister along with Miss Fuller for a river jaunt in his skiff. This time Miss Fuller seemed a school-girl gawky. When she snagged her pink sateen dress in an oarlock, Henry's face registered for his sister's benefit a comedy of exaggerated eye-rolling dismay unnoticed by their guest, who never stopped talking for a moment about a lecture she had attended the night before, not even when a length of sateen ripped into a kind of fringe that trailed into the water. At last catching her breath and looking about, she finally noticed the draggling finery and laughed easily, which made Anne like her after all. Then she quoted something in German and simpered and squinted, so she had liked her less. Naturally the laughing and the German, like everything else about her, were too loud for Henry.

As Henry headed down river on his own, Anne walked Miss Fuller back to the Emersons'.

"Please, do call me Margaret, as your brother does. And we have in common as well that we are both editors for Henry."

"No, I could not say I am his editor. I am a copyist, at times. We make the joke that I am his private secretary. We are all most grateful — I'm sure Henry is — that you have taken his pieces for *The Dial*."

"He has the soul of a poet, and I applaud his verses. But his essays, although rich and clear, are not, somehow, always *coherent*. I've only taken the one, you know. Sometimes his poet's soul *wanders*."

"Do you really think so."

They arrived at the garden gate. Anne flinched as the woman seemed about to embrace her; they settled for shaking hands.

Now she thought of her new Canary-bird, instantly thought to name her The Marchesa, then as quickly repenting of the joke, decided to call her plain Birdy instead. She would put the cage in the shade near the fields for the day, and find a tin cup for the bird's water. Two of the farmers, young brothers, would be scything and pitching hay today, and their sweat would plaster their shirts to the hard planes of their muscles. She tried to decide which was handsomer, Thomas or Robert. It would take further study.

The day grew lighter again. She urged the horses on, past

the tall green spears of mullein, the joe-pie weed with tight grey buds, the flutter of buttercups, campions, and hawk-weed that swayed and bobbed in the ditches by the road.

———

When Henry arrived in New York, a newspaper at the hotel carried the latest news of the wreck of the *Elizabeth*. She had foundered on a sand bar off Fire Island in the night three days earlier, in the freakishly violent hurricane that had run up the eastern coast, then cut across Long Island and into Connecticut, where it had abruptly died out into nothing more than heavy rains.

The paper was *The New York Globe* — a rival of Gree-ley's *Tribune* — and the tone of the article was dry. After reviewing the essentials — number of estimated dead in the nation (84), estimated speed of winds (more than 100 miles per hour), how many hurricanes reported on this path from previous years (3), number of merchant ships on the Atlantic estimated lost due to weather each year (27) — it focused on the continued efforts of the shipping company to recover their cargo, 150 tons of Carrera marble. She was a merchant vessel; apart from the crew and some livestock, the few passengers had included the writer Margaret Fuller, her two-year-old son, and her husband, the Italian marquis named Ossoli. All three, along with an Italian girl who was their maidservant, and two sailors, were now dead. Six dead, seventeen survived. The child's body had been found — he had died in the arms of a sailor only yards from the beach, and both bodies had already been buried behind the dunes. Now that the seas were calmer, rope lines and mule-teams would be engaged in the effort to drag the marble slabs to shore. The rest of the paper was filled with reports of the hurricane's wrecking path from the Carolinas north, and of the efforts to clean the streets of Manhattan from debris. A political cartoon showed the mayor of New York City riding the hurricane like a bucking horse. "Winds from Washington are powerful strong," he said.

In the *Tribune,* a black-bordered space offered a tribute to their dead correspondent. "Death of Margaret Fuller, the Marchesa Ossoli, the Most Famous Woman in the World," said the head-line. The next phrase continued editor Horace Greeley's combined instincts for drama and adver-tisement: "Tireless Champion of the Truth." Henry set the papers aside with a sigh.

That night Henry slept only a little, then rose early and walked through rubbishy streets. The mess of roof slates and broken glass was being cleaned by men with shovels and brooms. At the pier he caught a ferry to Bay Shore. The next ferry to Fire Island was delayed, so an oysterman with a single-sailed dory took him across the choppy bay.

He walked across the narrow finger of Fire Island in the hot, bright, salt-stung air. Dead animals, smashed cottages and barns, and flattened trees told of improbable disaster in the midst of rose-hips, sand, heather, thrushes. Coming up over the dunes to the ocean-side, he saw spread before him what looked like a battlefield: a tent encampment, teams of mules and drivers in the surf, the bulk of the destroyed ship so close to shore — absurd that it had sunk, that people had died, virtually on the beach! — and a line of slowly moving people stretched in either direction from the wreck as far as he could see. He realized that they were scavengers, pickers. Four days since the storm, only the dregs were left — shreds of soggy timber still peeling from the ship, bottles and ropes and bits of cloth that washed up. Important items, such as trunks and cartons and furniture, were long gone, he feared; unless perhaps the shipping company had done its own salvage work.

A short conversation with a boss at the mule-teams took away that hope. There was only one forlorn police-man guarding a sad heap of empty trunks wrested from the hands of pickers. Jumbled about were sea-weed, scraps of clothes, a couple of plates, a kettle, and a broken chair. The police-man held a brown goat on a leash of rope; the goat was browsing on the clothes.

"No one has claimed him," he said. "Do you want him?"

Henry said no. Once untied, the goat bounded off, first in the direction of the mules and then veering off into the dunes, chased by two determined pickers.

All that day Henry wandered the beach, speaking to the pickers and the sailors to see if they knew anything about the Ossolis' belongings, if they had seen any papers, but with no luck. The few surviving sailors now working on the marble crew were able to tell him more of the story.

The voyage of the *Elizabeth* had been troubled nearly from the first; soon after leaving Livorno on May 17th, the captain had died of typhus at Gibraltar. The ship sat in harbor under quarantine for a week, and then the first mate had taken charge. The Ossolis' boy then also came down with typhus, but a milder version than the captain's; he survived. Later, fierce winds hit just south of New York, and though the crew expected the mate to find a safe harbor and wait out the gale, he had pushed on.

Around three in the morning the ship, heavy with its marble cargo, had run aground on a sand bar. The marble slabs slid and thrust through the hull, and then the water poured in. Some five or six of the crew made it to shore by paddling on planks, and this was when the first unlucky sailor drowned. Those who landed on the beach were able to set up a make-shift tow-line, by which the rest of the crew and Mrs. Hasty, the late captain's wife, had struggled in — but the Italian girl had lost her grip on the rope and had been swept away in a rip current. The waves and wind were too loud to hear anyone scream, and the darkness was almost total.

Ossoli and his wife would not leave the ship without their son and the baby was of course too small to use the tow-line, or even to hold on to an adult. They were waiting for a promised life-boat from the nearest town. But instead of easing, the storm worsened; the tow-line broke; the ship broke up and began to sink. The ship was so close that those on shore saw clearly as Ossoli was next washed away. In the early dawn, a sailor actually swam back out to the wreck and took the child from his mother's arms and made for shore. Within minutes, he and the boy had been beaten and killed in the ferocious surf, pulled back again and again by the undertow. Then the woman was alone, most of her skirts torn away, sitting with her back pressed against the mast, her knees at her chin. Finally an enormous wave covered her as well and she disappeared.

One sailor told Henry how much the crew had liked the lady, how she had expertly nursed the sick captain and a sailor at Gibraltar early in the voyage and then had nursed her own son without panic. Past the Canaries, once the boy was out of danger, she became sociable; one night, she joined the crew below and told them the story of Aeneas and the founding of Rome. For many nights thereafter, he said, she had told stories from Virgil, with long pauses to allow for translation for the Italian men in the crew — for although she did speak some Italian, they had laughed at her accent and formal style and so she had wisely stayed with English.

"Dido's death by fire," said Henry thinking suddenly, vividly, of the way Margaret had sometimes looked at Emerson.

"She could tell a story! Waving her arms, she had a beautiful voice, she looked like an angel. The boy sitting on her lap just stared up at her face."

Another sailor, Bolton, whose good pal had tried to save the child, showed Henry to the small grave-yard and its scrap-wood crosses. "We have to keep the pickers away from here or they'd take these too, for fire-wood." Bolton was talking too much, still had a shocked look about the eyes, as he told of the mother handing her child into the sailor's arms. "The husband was gone under already, but she held the boy above the water and handed him to Tomaso. We yelled on the beach, we called to the little boy and brave old Tommy — 'Come on, come on! The lady will try for it, too!'

"And then we all — us on the beach and she on the ship — we saw them go under. Between the wreck and the beach, tossed and smashed, Tommy and the little boy. It wasn't till morning, when the rips had calmed, that the bodies came close enough for us to drag them in, dead. She saw everything, her boy drowned in the sailor's arms. She never moved after that.

"We watched her, her legs tucked up under her petticoats, gazing at the place where her son had gone under, she sat still as stone, until the waves took her too and knocked her sideways and she went over and under."

A few other sailors and salvage workers brought their lunches up to the hill and sat with them at the graves. Someone gave Henry a piece of bread, some cheese, and a sour plum. They chewed and they drank cider from a common jug, and then they and Bolton resumed their talk, which seemed to be, over and over to one another: "Terrible storm, worst ever, terrible voyage, bad seas, fool captain, bad luck, marble too heavy, slid right through the hold, never go on a merchant again carrying stone if I can help it."

Henry thought he could hardly bear to hear it again but each of the sailors seemed to need to say it, more than once, and so it became a kind of muttered chorus: "Terrible storm, bodies lost forever, the child tossed and tossed, brave lady, the child, terrible terrible sea."

Ellery Channing and Arthur Fuller arrived just before sunset. The scale of the mess at the beach nearly overwhelmed them; but in an unmethodical manner, they more or less retraced Henry's search all that evening, with identical results. There was brief excitement when Ellery found some scraps of paper in a note-book — upon drying them, however, they could see enough of the lettering to make out that these were only pieces of the ship's log. Camping out near the workers, without a tent, they had tried to cheer one another but a light rain kept their gloom constant through the night. In the morning Arthur oversaw the digging up of his nephew's coffin and hired a cart for the first leg of its trip back to Cambridge for family burial. Since it seemed that all hope of recovering the other bodies was gone, they spoke about the missing manuscript instead. It was Margaret's book, her "History of the Italian Revolution." Her last letters home had announced its completion. There was little chance, they knew, of finding it — but Henry made a promise as Arthur and Ellery left with their burden, that he would continue to try.

Richard Fuller, Margaret's youngest brother and Henry's good friend, had stayed behind in Boston with a fever. More than for anyone else, Henry wanted to recover something for Richard. All he had were two jet buttons from a coat, perhaps Ossoli's, that he had found on a scrap of wool cloth in the foam.

Henry resumed his beach walking. He was looking now for nothing in particular, and was able to enjoy noting the dozens of sea-birds, their fishing habits and cries; kelp and sea-lettuce and small moon-jellies pulsing on the sand; the razor clam-shells and jingle-shells and acres of boat-shells, lumpy underfoot.

A few miles down from the salvage encampment, as he was stepping idly along the wave line, he put a foot directly onto a mass of kelp and bones. They were big bones, and not of fish — he looked closely and saw that they were not quite clean-picked by the gulls and crabs, and definitely human — a shoulder, and an arm, two fingers still attached with shreds of cartilage. He could not touch these bones. No doubt they were from the wreck. They could be from any one of the bodies. He believed nonetheless that they were Margaret's. That looked like her hand, it did, feminine, with her long fingers.

He thought perhaps of taking a finger bone for Richard. It was like something out of a fairy tale, but what? The Seven Crow Brothers, that was the one — with the sister who saved them all by whittling her own finger into a key to fit an impossible lock. . . . And yet he could not touch the bones. Instead he took off his boots and used them as scoops, scraping up wet sand and burying the bones as best he could; then, barefoot, carrying the boots, he walked back quickly, the red light from the setting sun in his eyes.

———

Even before life had been disrupted by the ship-wreck, things in the Thoreau house that summer were already in a state of agitation ("all of a doo-dah," said Mother) because the family was packing to move, to a large house they had recently completed building in the center of town. This was a social and economic "return," as their move out of town several years earlier had marked a grim moment in their finances. The family's move back to the center of Concord was made possible by the recent prosperity of their pencil factory. This small business, which Father had inherited, occupied a barn warehouse. The family had always joked about their move "west" a half mile from town, and called the house-and-barn their "Texas" house. Henry's inventions — of a new way of grinding plumbago for pencil lead and for printing, and a new way of pressing the wood together around the lead — had made the business thrive, so that now they were providing pencils and printer's ink to shops throughout New England and even Europe. Once they had moved back "east" into the center of town, their old Texas house would serve as offices and shipping station for the business.

But with Henry away, the moving had slowed. Mother was in a stew, un-packing and re-wrapping the plate and glassware, so that dozens of bundles littered the dining-room and parlor. All meals were now eaten in the kitchen. Father was not good at asking for help and kept trying to do the heavy work by himself; last night, the fourth day of Henry's absence, he had strained his back trying to move a grain bin.

Anne was down to one smock, one dress, and a shift — everything else was packed away in trunks. For now most of Henry's things were temporarily lodged in a shed, and there Anne hung the bird-cage and, every morning, tended to his Monarch caterpillars. He had allowed her to help with his butterfly hatchery this year — last year, his first of documenting, she only had been allowed to watch. She was better than he, it turned out, at finding the rice-like white eggs on the milkweed plants. Of the dozen or so they had captured in June, only five had hatched into caterpillars, and one was now so fat it would soon be at its last moult and go into a chrysalid.

That morning, when Mother was rubbing Father's back with liniment and scolding him, Anne escaped the kitchen and went out to the shed for her morning chore. She peered into the glass box that sat on the table by the one window, then lifted the pierced-tin lid with great delicacy — the fresh, shiny green chrysalid was attached by sticky threads to the underside of a pierced dimple — and reached in to drop fresh milkweed leaves for the caterpillars that were still eating. She fished out the dried leaves and with a rag pinched up the tiny black droppings.

She and her brother shared a sort of giddy admiration for these plump caterpillars, striped like a dandy's waist-coat out of *The Lady's Book* in bright yellow-green, black, and white. When you held one in your hand, it would at first curl up timidly, its wedges of caterpillar flesh bunched together like a squashed accordion; but then it would stretch out again, lifting its head and waggling short black horns.

The tabby cat had followed Anne to the shed. She nosed against the glass box, then against Anne's pencil and ruler, and got a vigorous push off the table. The Canary-bird twittered nervously. In the Monarchs note-book, Anne wrote a description of the chrysalid, gently angling the ruler for a measurement. She then measured and noted, to a millimetre's precision, the length of each caterpillar. A cloth tailor's tape with millimetre markings went around the thickest place on each one — for a "waist" measurement, circumference. She wrote it all down and dated it. Then she made several preliminary sketches. Henry was in correspondence with a Dr. Jaeger, who was compiling an encyclopedia of insects; their data would be mailed to him. Possibly Anne's drawings would be included in the encyclopedia. She was exact in detail, but her perspective and shading were inexpert and Henry argued with her about her choice of colors. She hoped he would remember to buy her some new watercolor paints in New York.

It was necessary to push the cat off the table again. She tidied the note-books, then replaced the lid, anchored it with stones, and shooed the cat ahead of her. She looked idly at the piles of Henry's books and noticed, suddenly, a thin green-bound volume with gilt lettering: *Woman in the Nineteenth Century* by Margaret Fuller. She had never read it. Well. She would read it now. Was it a coincidence that she had found it, or was it that her eyes were newly alert to the author's name? She tucked it into the front pocket of her smock and closed the shed door.

A surprise: Miss Fuller's brother Arthur had stopped in, and he would stay for a cup of tea. Father sat stiffly by the stove, his face drawn, but fortunately Mother was occupied with the visitor and had let up her scolding. Arthur Fuller looked wild, his big hands clumsy, his pale eyes flat and full of the ocean at which he had been staring. His sister's body was not recovered — nor was her husband's, nor the book — just some scraps of clothing. He nearly broke into tears many times. He told them about the one recovered body — that of his nephew, little Angelo Ossoli, not yet two years old, for whom a grave in the upper dunes had been quickly dug the day after the wreck. "I never saw his face in life," said Arthur. "I never met my nephew. There was a wooden cross — we dug it all up and brought him back in a crate."

The funeral for his nephew would be held the next day in Boston; Arthur was to visit with Mr. Emerson briefly before heading back to be with his own family. He gave Anne a note from her brother.

> Dear Annie,
> There are difficulties and we will probably not succeed in finding what we came for. I am staying for a week or so more to walk and hunt for specimens. Tell Mother. I have notes on birds and other beach life and will bring you shells and a skate's egg-sac called a devil's purse. It is empty, but do not let that give you false comfort. The devil grows richer every day.
>
> H.

———

Henry hired the oysterman to take him to Mattituck, on the North Fork of Long Island. He spent several days there, boarding with a farmer, and continued his walks and his notes. On his last day, he returned to Fire Island and watched the dogged, nearly finished haulage of the marble.

Most of the stone was in rough slabs, but there were also two out-sized marble statues, a man standing and a man on a horse, lying, bizarrely, on the sand. By looking more closely, he realized that the block faces had been left unsculpted — evidently these stone figures were basic models of the heroic, meant to be adapted locally once they had reached their destinations, some county seat court-house, some new library or athenaeum in Ohio or Maryland. They shared the feature of having the right arm raised. The solitary man pointed to an indefinite future — for the moment, as he reclined on the wet sand, to the clouds above the beach. The figure on horseback had suffered more from the wreck: The horse's neck and head were gone and the man's extended arm was broken off at the elbow, making his intended gesture less clear.

The police-man had vanished, and so had the pickers. But the sailor Bolton dropped his work and came over to tell Henry that one of the locals had been offering something for sale, papers he thought, from the wreck. He directed him to a fishing shack which stood close by the grave-yard.

———

The family had decided that no further moving could take place until Henry was home. In the lull, Anne visited the widow Allan at her two-room shack down by the creek, where she tended her vegetable garden and took in washing and mending. Dolly Allan's own children were grown and gone, and she had worked for the family as house-maid and nurse-maid when Anne was little. Anne had tried for years to educate her; and although she no longer tried, she still read to her.

That day she brought with her Margaret Fuller's *Woman in the Nineteenth Century*. As she held the delicate volume in her hand, she thought how much more discreet and seemly than its author the object was. Dolly was pulling weeds; Anne set down her book and basket — which contained a thick slice of ham, a loaf of bread, and a cup of cream as well as a jar of lemonade — and bent to help her.

Inside, they put the food away. Anne opened the jar and poured the lemonade into cups as Dolly washed at the sink pump. They settled into their usual postures: Anne with the book on a cushion on the floor, Dolly sitting on a chair behind her, embracing her with her knees. The old woman unpinned and unbraided the young woman's light brown hair. As Anne read, Dolly combed and stroked, dipped her comb into rose-petal water, combed the hair through, braided it, unbraided it, twisted it up and pinned it, then unpinned it and combed it some more. Anne propped her elbow on Dolly's knee; the older woman's cotton skirt was patterned with green sprigs, faded to the same hue as the book.

Woman in the Nineteenth Century had made Miss Fuller famous. It had made it possible for her to go to England, where the book had excited admiration; and to France and Italy, where it had appeared in translations almost immediately. But Anne had never read it. She found that the style took some getting used to. She thought, as she paused occasionally to make sense of what she had just read aloud, that it was not exactly flowery — but rather somehow vegetal, vine-like, even mouldy, each sentence adhering around some central idea, with examples.

> In clear triumphant moments, many times, has rung through the spheres the prophecy of his [man's] jubilee, and those moments, though past in time, have been translated into eternity by thought; the bright signs they left hang in the heavens, as single stars or constellations, and, already, a thickly sown radiance consoles the wanderer in the darkest night. Other heroes since Hercules have fulfilled the zodiac of beneficient labors, and then given up their mortal part to the fire without a murmur; while no God dared deny that they should have their reward.

Miss Fuller began with an invocation of Man's capacity for the heroic, and went on to explain that Man cannot be fully heroic until Woman is allowed to be heroic beside him. In her first intimation of the main argument, she wrote of women that:

> Those who till a spot of earth scarcely larger than
> is wanted for a grave, have deserved that the sun
> should shine upon its sod till violets answer.

Anne looked up from the book and said, "That's elegant. It sounds a lot like Henry."

"All done?" asked Dolly, making a final twist and pinning Anne's hair back into place.

"It goes on forever, actually. I'll bring something more lively next time. You need your nap."

She settled Dolly on her low bed.

"How is the moving coming along?" Dolly asked.

"Hectic — Mother throwing her hands in the air and shouting, and Father trying to pull the stove out of the wall. We hope Henry will come home soon to supervise."

"You need a home of your own."

"I know I do," said Anne. "But I almost feel that I shouldn't. Helen and John never had the chance to marry. Henry and Sissy — they both say they will never marry."

"But you must."

It was too hot for a blanket, even with all the shutters closed against the sun. Anne kissed the old woman's cheek and smoothed her sparse white hair.

"I'll do your hair next time." It was an old joke.

"If you undo it, it will fly away."

Back at home, Anne returned to the book with reluctance. Guilt about her dislike of Margaret — would she call her Margaret at last, now that she was dead? — made her disinclination to wade through those sentences feel like an actual crime. So she would read.

Miss Fuller argued for the need to explore the full capacities of both men and women. Ah, this was familiar. She acknowledged that most women would continue to be womanly, and interested in domestic affairs; but she also maintained that in such a time as this nineteenth century, when women have unjustly lost much liberty by having lost their property rights (such as they had known in early centuries and in different cultures), it behooved more women to turn to what she termed their "Minerva" side. Minerva again! Minerva represented the wise, masculine aspect of femininity. By allowing Minerva to flourish, she said, women could accomplish a redress of the bad bargain that currently prohibited women from exploring their male strengths (of leadership, courage, invention), or men from exploring their female strengths (of kindness, spirituality, nurturance). This was exactly the same language of the Conversations. But the next passage went further:

> We would have every arbitrary barrier thrown down. We would have every path laid open to woman as freely as to man. . . . We believe the divine energy would pervade nature to a degree unknown in the history of former ages, and that no discordant collision, but a ravishing harmony of the spheres would ensue. . . .

The sexes should not only correspond to and appreciate, but prophesy to one another. In individual instances this happens. Two persons love in one another the future good which they aid one another to unfold. . . .

When Emily Plater [a hero of the Polish independence movement] joined the army where the reports of her exploits preceded her . . . some of the officers were disappointed at her quiet manners; that she had not the air and tone of a stage-heroine. They thought she could not have acted heroically unless in buskins; had no idea that such deeds only showed the habit of her mind.

Others talked of the delicacy of her sex, advised her to withdraw from perils and dangers, and had no comprehension of the feelings within her breast that made this impossible. . . . But though, to the mass of these men, she was an embarrassment and a puzzle, the nobler sort viewed her with a tender enthusiasm worthy of her. . . .

Mercy! She closed the book; she would help fix supper. Sieving the creamed potato soup — Anne had proposed they try it cold in the French way — she asked Mother and Sissy if they had ever heard of Emily Plater. Mother said, as she had often before: "Women and war are an abominable combination. Joan of Arc — or your Emily Plater — are stories to sicken any woman of right feeling." She slammed the stove door for emphasis. Whatever the weather, they would have the biscuits hot.

That night, unable to sleep in the heat, Anne felt herself still whirling inside what she had read. She was wearied by the tortured way that Fuller's argument ranged, without apparent logic or — well, control. What was it about the philosophers (she excepted Henry of course, and anyway he disdained the label) that made them argue in circles, moreover in circles that kept expanding indefinitely? It was as if they were looping out into the future, including everyone now and forever. She lit the candle and continued to read.

> The electrical, the magnetic element in woman has not been fairly brought out in any period. Every thing might be expected from it; she has far more of it than man. This is commonly expressed by saying that her intuitions are more rapid and more correct. . . .
>
> Women who combine this with creative genius, are very commonly unhappy at present. They see too much to act in conformity with those around them. . . .
>
> Those, who seem overladen with electricity,

frighten those around them. . . . Woe to such a woman who finds herself linked to a [petty] man in bonds too close. It is the cruelest of errors. He will detest her with all the bitterness of wounded self-love. He will take the whole prejudice of manhood upon himself, and to the utmost of his power imprison and torture her by its imperious rigors.

Now the writer was getting angry; her prose was jabbing at the reader. She gave examples of electrical women — Iphigenia, Cassandra — who frightened men and so were killed off.

I observe in [Cassandra's] case, and in one known to me here, that, what might have been a gradual and gentle disclosure of remarkable powers, was broken and jarred into disease by an unsuitable marriage.

You ask, what use will [woman] make of liberty, when she has so long been sustained and restrained?

Anne liked that — the false logic of sound, as if *sustained* and *restrained* were inseparable; the one the price of the other. Or perhaps the logic was not false.

> . . . If you ask me what offices she may fill; I reply
> — any. I do not care what case you put; let them
> be sea-captains, if you will.

"Sea-captains!" Anne said it aloud.

> I do not doubt there are women well fitted for
> such an office, and if so, I should be glad to see
> them in it . . .
> I wish woman to live, first for God's sake.
> Then she will not make an imperfect man her
> god, and thus sink to idolatry. . . . A profound
> thinker has said, "no married woman can repre-
> sent the female world, for she belongs to her
> husband. The idea of woman must be repre-
> sented by a virgin."

It was not clear to Anne if the "profound thinker" was
Emerson, or possibly Carlyle or Goethe. But the Free
Woman must resist all male gods, all male authorities,
including her own father and her husband:

> But that is the very fault of marriage, and of the
> present relation between the sexes, that woman
> does belong to the man, instead of forming a
> whole with him. . . . It is a vulgar error . . .

(Was she calling Emerson vulgar?)

> . . . that love, a love, to woman is her whole
> existence; she also is born for Truth and Love
> in their universal energy. . . . I know that I, a
> daughter, live through the life of man; but what
> concerns me now is, that my life be a beautiful,
> powerful, in a word, a complete life of its kind.

That was the clear end, the major crashing chord, of the essay. Although Miss Fuller threw in a bad poem treacled with high sentiments to close, Anne held to the phrase *a complete life of its kind* and knew she would not forget it.

The awkward, herky-jerky force of the essay, rather like an electric eel, twisting, brilliant, sparking — that, and the heat-lightning flashing and filling the window-panes — kept her awake until the dawn.

———

Henry returned in a thunder-storm. A crate of specimens came off the cart with him.

As Sissy made tea in the nearly empty kitchen Anne told Henry about the Monarchs — one had already taken wing; three more were still in chrysalid state; one pouch had fallen, black and dead, to the bottom of the case. The kitchen table and nearly all the china had gone to the new house, so they set their tea-cups, without saucers, on the broad lip of the stove. The rain stopped and the sun came through the dripping window of the kitchen. Henry excused himself to go take tea with the Emersons. Lidian, Mrs. E, had sent a note asking him to come right away.

"He has gone to his Maker," said Anne to her sister.

"I don't enjoy your jokes about Mr. E," Sissy said.

"You mean God?"

"It is not amusing."

"I will call him Jove, then, is that better?"

Henry walked the short path to the Emersons', and at the gate Lidian saw him coming and rushed to embrace him. She was sniffing; he backed away so as not to encourage any real tears. Mr. E was in his study, but he was no longer morose. He was talking and pacing, almost preaching, to Ellery Channing, who seemed to be taking notes. "Henry! Ellery told me you had stayed to scavenge."

"I was collecting specimens, yes."

Henry then noticed James Freeman Clarke, standing over by the corner window, and they bowed slightly to one another. His reddish hair, backlit by the late afternoon sun, stood out in wisps from his pale head. *Clarke looks like an old man*, Henry thought. Years ago many of them had guessed he might marry Margaret; but Lidian had thought not, and she had been right.

Emerson said, "We are beginning — embarking — you know, Ellery is really the man in charge, on a book of memoirs of Margaret, selections of her own writings accompanied by recollections of those who knew her best — myself, Ellery, Clarke, Greeley — commemorating her genius."

He paused, then announced: "'Memoirs of Margaret Fuller Ossoli.' You must contribute as well. Collecting her best words. Commemorating her genius."

Henry took tea and sandwiches and waited for the others to leave. James inquired after Henry's studies and said that while he was staying in town he would like to accompany him on a botanising walk or a river jaunt. Henry looked at James's sleek brown boots and gave his usual shuffling answer about it all depending on the weather. Mr. E ate greedily and needed help to push his chair back from the table — one could not help but notice the girth he had added recently. Standing up to his nearly six full feet, however, he seemed in fine proportion.

After tea he and Henry took one of their usual paths, through the orchard and then on up the hill for a good view. Mr. E talked without ceasing about Margaret, her peculiar genius, her radical habits of mind, her place in the history of thought and action. Suddenly he sat down hard on a mossy rock, interrupting his own monologue, and softly wailed —

"Oh, have I done wrong?"

"What? Tell me."

Mr. E did not want to go on; or he did, but he couldn't. He pouted out his lips like a child. Henry was patient, staring out at the heavy trees that clustered along the curving river in the distance. The crown of one of the trees was yellower than the others — a hickory?

"I — I advised — I refused. She wanted money, months ago — she begged me for a loan and I did not answer, and she wrote to Greeley for an advance from the *Tribune*, for the book on the revolution — and I was in New York with Greeley at the time. He was short of ready money in any case, and I advised him not to make the sacrifice."

Horace Greeley, founder and editor of the *New-York Daily Tribune*, was Margaret's employer and champion. She had written dozens and dozens of dispatches from Europe for him, all these years. He had published *Woman in the Nineteenth Century* and had promised to publish her book on the Italian revolution. Greeley and his wife and children were Margaret's dear friends. This was incredible.

"Not to send her money he planned to pay her anyway?" Henry said.

"Not even a portion of it. I feared — we all feared — she would never come home. Such rumors we had been hearing, you know them yourself, from the Springs and that portrait painter — Ricks? Hicks? — and Hawthorne's friend, the one who knows the Brownings. . . ."

"I did not believe the rumors," said Henry stiffly. "If they did not have a marriage in a Protestant church that does not mean they were not married."

"But marriage itself has been doubted, amongst people who knew —"

"Everyone would have doubted the marriage if it were in the Roman church as well. She explained all that, you told me yourself. They were married in late autumn of 1847, but the records were lost in the subsequent confusion of the war. These speculations are ridiculous and mean-spirited."

"I confess I was at first shocked that she had married at all." Two tiny green grass-hoppers leapt up from the grass and clung to Mr. E's trouser leg. He brushed them away and continued:

"The domestic life, as wife and mother, always seemed to me something Margaret was too — noble, I think, yes, too noble for. She had too pure an intellect and character to . . . but the rumors —"

"We need not listen to slander," Henry said.

"The only way to counter slander was for her and her husband and baby to come home, so we could see them all."

Henry walked on ahead, to an old apple-tree that had just recently broken in two. The place where the break had happened was pale and mealy, and the center was hollow where the tree had been rotting from within. He plucked a green apple no bigger than a quail's egg and polished it in his hands as Mr. E caught up.

"Are you angry, Henry?"

"Did you even think about how they would live here? On what income? Would her brothers have taken them in?"

"Or Elizabeth Peabody, or I. Our hands would have been open, once she was home. We would have found a place for them in Concord, or with her mother. Elizabeth proposed she begin a new series of Conversations. And naturally her book on the revolution would have been published. "

"Do you know if she asked anyone else for money?" asked Henry.

"Her brothers. I think they had already sent her what they could spare. And she did ask Elizabeth, too. I told her not to send money, either. I persuaded her that Margaret must come home."

Henry said, "You took a lot upon yourself."

"It was for her own good! I know it was! But — I saw her brother Richard yesterday in Boston. He had only just received a letter she wrote in May, from Livorno, as they were waiting to board. A letter from the dead! Poor thing, he's been ill enough. In the letter she wrote that they had borrowed money for food and boat fare, and that they were nearly starved."

"No."

"And that the only fare home they could afford was on a merchant ship. They could not even afford the packet boat, which would have been safer — so many merchant ships are lost, so dangerous with the baby — And on another boat, they would have arrived much earlier. Don't you see? And avoided the storm!"

Mr. E groaned and rubbed his face.

If sin existed, this was a sin; but who could grant absolution? Henry only said, "You could not have known."

On their silent walk back down the hill, Henry absent-mindedly handed the green apple to Mr. E. He as absently took a little bite, then quickly spat it out and tossed the bitter fruit into the grass.

Henry had a sudden memory of one summer, many years earlier, when Margaret had come for her usual stay at the Emersons' home. He had been living there too, as he often did, working as a carpenter and general handy-man in the house and garden in exchange for the peace of his study-hours at a desk in the barn. He was short of money then, and the Emersons were kind to him. Margaret had joined them in July, to Henry's mild annoyance — she took up all of Mr. E's best conversation, and seemed as well to make Lidian nervous.

But what he now remembered was something else: her quick look of sympathy that day when Mr. E had folded some coins in a paper and shoved it at him through the breakfast cups. It was called a "loan" but was really a gift; she knew so; she also knew that Henry must have needed it, and that he hated to receive it in front of her. The next week, she had bought two poems of his for *The Dial* — poems he knew for a certainty she did not like, he could tell well enough — and paid him more than he supposed poems usually merited. He angrily questioned her "charity," she as angrily insisted it was nothing of the kind, and if he thought it was charity, well, he could give it to a charitable cause. So he did; the ten dollars she had paid him he gave to the First Parish Church fund for the new steeple.

"Since then," said Margaret, who liked to repeat her own jokes, "I always think of you when I hear the bell. *The Dial* paid the *toll*."

It was a hard thing to need money, to have to ask for it. It might also be a hard thing to give it; but Mr. E and Greeley and the others had not, in this case, done that particular hard thing.

The light was low and the shadows long when they arrived at the back door of the Emersons' house. Henry did not go inside, and he took his old friend's hand in his.

"It *was* right that she should come home," said Henry. "It's contrary for any American to live in Europe. She needed to come home." He meant those words; he was not lying. But he held some other words back.

Mr. E rubbed again at his face, making the skin ruddy and disarranging his side-whiskers, and heavily climbed the back steps. Henry found that he was not able to tell him about what he had discovered on Fire Island. Emerson was a man with money to give or not to give. He and Margaret were mice who darted for crumbs.

———

The family finished the move into the new house. Two horses and a sledge were hired to drag the last heavy pieces: Henry's work-table, Mother's stove, the storage bins, and the wardrobes. Henry was to have the attic to himself, but neither of its doors was large enough for his enormous ancient table. He had to saw off the legs first and then, with two other men helping, he and Father carried up the top. He then installed some hardware screws in the legs, and Anne helped him twist the legs back into the augered holes he had made in the top. He fretted the entire time about the danger of the wood top splitting, as it was very old cherry — and his sister as always was patient. She swept up the shavings into her hand as he re-drilled one of the holes. He did not look up from his work when he told her he had something to show her from his trip.

The table was up, the wood had not cracked, the legs were steady. They pushed it into place under the west window. Then Henry hoisted the crate onto the table and pried off the top slats as Anne collected into a tidy pile the confetti of straw that fluttered out. She held up a piece with drooping seeds that bobbed like a feather.

"It's called sand-oats," said Henry. "It covers the dunes."

First came out the present of the new box of paints, not only small blocks of water-colors, but plump packets of powder for mixing with oil as well, including a new white called "Clear White," Indian Yellow, and Persian Green.

"Lovely! Oh, Henny!"

"You said you wanted to learn oil techniques — here's a little book about mixing the oils and making the palette, and painting on proper canvases. I can stretch some for you on frames if you like."

Then some shells, several of the skate's egg-sacs he had promised — they looked like enormous black beetles with horns on both ends — and drift-wood, sea-polished stones, sea-gull feathers, and smelly pieces of kelp came out of the crate. There was still something large under the straw, which Henry now gently swept off with his hand. He pulled the large box out.

It was a lap-desk, made of pine or some other deal-wood, with blonde fruit-wood veneer badly damaged. A green square of tooled leather, held down by dimpled bronze carpet tacks, had cracked and peeled away in strips from the slant top; the bronze latch was loose because, Henry explained, a picker had pried it open with a knife. As Anne looked over his shoulder, he lifted the lid: inside was a spilt-out bottle of brownish ink and a huge stain, like dried blood, that covered the bottom of the desk box. A pen with its nib missing, the cork to the ink bottle, some blotting scraps, a button, a litter of sand and shells, and several drawing-pins rattled about. And there was a well-stained pile of manuscript pages, covered in large writing.

Carefully, she reached in and picked up the pages — the bottom sheaf stuck to the wood, and as she pulled it up, it tore slightly and left a smudged shadow of paper. It seemed that all these were pages of a letter, a private letter, addressed to "Sophie." At the very top, in urgent block letters, was written: **IF FOUND, THIS LETTER IS FOR SOPHIA HAWTHORNE IN CONCORD MASSACHUSETTS. M.F.**

OSSOLI. Similar printing was partly visible through the ink stain on the bottom page as well: DEAR SOPHIE, THE SHIP [BLOT] IF [BLOT] TOW [BLOT] PRAY MY NINO [BLOT] NOT FRIGHT [BLOT]. 18 JU [BLOT] LO [BLOT] M.

"Have you read it?" she asked her brother.

"No, how can you ask? It's for Mrs. Hawthorne."

She placed the papers carefully back in the desk. "It says 'Concord' — she must not have known they moved to the Berkshire hills. Did Miss Fuller write to you, ever, from Europe?"

"Once or twice. I have the last one here — I just got it out of my piles of papers yesterday."

It was dated June of 1849. "Rome was under siege by French troops when she wrote this," said Henry as he handed it to her.

> Dear Henry,
> Horace has sent me 3 of the 5 installments in <u>Sartain's Union Magazine</u> of your astonishing account of hiking the woods in the north & climbing magnificent Ktaadn. It is likely he sent me all 5, tho' I received but 3; the mail here is frightfully uneven because of the war — or, I should say, <u>wars</u>, as they arise across the Continent. (We have hopes yet for Poland!) I hear in your voice the voice of home, the voice of the pine-trees themselves, in these sentences — they are a thrill-

ing testament to your deepest soul, to what you call the Wild. There is an altogether different mood here, dear Henry, the chaos of hope turned to despair & betrayal. All is going very badly with the Revolution as you know if you read my dispatches. We are under daily bombardment, & the spectre of death is everywhere. But we cannot lose faith in the rising star of Liberty, calling to the Good Wildness within us all — Wild Liberty that answers from soul to soul, that will knit us into a better, voluntary society of free men & women. I hear so little news of home — Mr E has not written once since his visit last year to England, when he did not venture south to see me, after all — & I miss you all & the peace & concord of Concord. But my spirit has found its sphere of action, its call to witness. Please, please, dear Henry, write to me & give me your news. In haste, Your sincere friend,

MF

"I didn't write back," said Henry. "I was cross with her about not understanding. About the Wild. She was always mis-using my words and the words of others, bending them to her own meanings."

"Something no one else has ever done."

"Well yes, of course — I can't think why it irked me so."

"It's all right, Henry." Anne touched the lines of writing on the page delicately. "I like her hand. It's so grand and forceful! Not the least bit lady-like, I'm afraid."

"She was short-sighted. I think that's why she wrote such a large hand."

Anne held up Henry's letter next to the one in the desk. "A letter is a very *live* thing, isn't it?"

"When I went over to see Jove, the day I came home, I meant to talk to him about the desk and the letter to Mrs. Hawthorne. Somehow I thought he might like to deliver the letter and visit the Hawthornes with me."

"I could go! I want to see the mountains —"

"But I never even told him about this letter. It was strange. I couldn't."

He told Anne about Emerson's planned "Memoirs" and also about the money that had never been sent to the Ossolis.

"Were they punishing her?" Anne asked.

"I don't think so. They wanted her to come home. We all wanted that."

"Indeed. I'm afraid I don't see why." Anne was surprised to find herself taking Miss Fuller's part. "No one wanted her to marry an Italian, so they wouldn't want to meet him either, would they?"

"They wanted everything to be proper — up to standard. It would be best for the child," said Henry.

"He was an Italian child, wouldn't he be best living in Italy?"

"He was also American. All Americans are best living here."

She rubbed the tabby's head, those two almost-bald spots in front of her ears. A purr rumbled out, but then Anne clutched the cat so close she struggled and jumped free with a squawk.

"Can I go with you to see the Hawthornes?"

"I need to write to them first."

Henry wrote the letter that day. It was another week before the reply arrived.

In that week, at a picnic, Anne decided which of the two farming brothers she preferred: It was Thomas, the elder. She said nothing to Mother or Sissy, but she did tell Dolly Allan.

"How do you know you like him best?"

"He is going to have the farm when his father dies, and Henry likes talking to him about threshers and rotation and all the advanced ideas for farming. He admires Henry and he is the *only* person I've ever seen Henry explain his pencil inventions to — the ground plumbago, you know, for printing. Henry says Thomas is a 'coming man.' He also likes my drawings."

"I don't suppose he's at all handsome."

"So he is! You know he is! And he smells wonderful."

"Annie!"

"He does — like hay and burnt toast. And sometimes peppermint."

Lenox, 18th August '50.

My dear Henry,

Glad as we must always be to hear from you, this occasion tests even that felicity. Mrs. Hawthorne has been saddened by the death of "La Signora Ossoli," as have I. We offer up our condoling to the crêpe and grosgrain of mourning in which all Concord doubtless has draped herself since the news of her daughter's final fall.

However, that is "as far as it goes" — as the good pig farmer who lives down the road says. This Berkshire Hog will not go a-snuffling in the dirt to snout out scrips and scraps.

To put it plainly: Neither my wife nor I has any wish to receive, and most certainly will not read, the letter you describe. Do oblige me by disposing of it in the nearest stove. I can only wish you had not troubled to fish it out from the sea.

Do you think me harsh? No doubt you do not know the worst of what we know, of her irregular life, in Italy and before. In our days in Concord, she was merely a Transcendental heifer, and tho' we were fond of her as one of our own and endured her posturings as those of a sister, the wide world showed her for what she truly was. There was a Jew in New York who made her his mistress, on good authority. As for Italy, you all may trick up as a legitimate, even aristocratic, marriage and family this disgraceful business, of a bastard child fathered on her by an Italian rowdy with a fantastic name, but I shall not join you. She would have done better to have gone over to Rome entirely and entered a nunnery. Foolish Ophelia.

Thrice in recent months I have been obliged to intercept letters from that woman to my wife. With her permission — and her tender heart made her give it at first with difficulty — I have destroyed them unread.

When next I hear from you, I hope it will be on a topic more inclined to foster our mutual friendship. By all means visit our hovel in the hills, provided you come empty-handed.

N. Hawthorne

"My goodness," Anne said. "This is a shocking thing." She handed the letter back to her brother. "I suppose he also means to be amusing. But I don't understand. Surely Miss Fuller was their friend?"

"I don't know," he said miserably. "She was their friend, once — I thought they were all quite taken with one another. I often don't understand these things. I thought she admired his writing, even to excess. Whatever could she have said, or done? I know that he is an anti-revolutionist, but I am surprised that he would let a difference of opinion affect an old friendship. . . ."

"Mother says he is actually opposed to Abolition!"

"It's not so simple," Henry said. "Hawthorne despises slavery, just as he despises tyranny, but he also despairs. He thinks revolutions and Abolition are doomed enterprises — get rid of one form of slavery, and another will take its place — and so he mocks us all for hoping."

"What will you do with the letter?"

"What he says — get rid of it," said Henry.

"But it is addressed to *her*, and *she* does not say that."

"I suppose I could send it, and let him do what he likes —"

The Canary-bird's cage hung in the attic's east window. Anne poked a finger in, preened the bird's head, and let it gnaw the finger delicately.

"What he likes may not be what she likes," she said, "and in any case obviously he takes charge of their correspondence. I don't think you should do anything with it now. Maybe in a few years he will soften, or she will write herself and ask for it."

"I am uncomfortable having it around. It feels like a corpse, or like something stolen."

"These are her Last Words." She said it with the capitals.

"She wrote thousands and thousands of words, far too many words, one might say. I don't want to be burdened, like a ghostly postman. *Margaret's* ghost's postman, I mean."

"I read *Woman in the Nineteenth Century*. She does go

on, but I thought parts of it were wonderful. 'Let them be sea-captains, if they will!'"

"Do you want to be a sea-captain?" said Henry.

"Certainly not. Ow!" The bird pecked too hard, and she pulled out her finger to suck it. "I want to paint and make botanical drawings and have seven children and when I go on a sea voyage, I hope the captain will be a good strong man who will keep me safe. But I still like that she wrote it. It's a grand dream." She wrinkled up her brow, almost comically, and then said, "But that's a terrible tragic irony, isn't it, that she was ship-wrecked? And *that* captain was a man."

"Women are never logical." Henry looked at Hawthorne's letter again, puzzling. "Perhaps she didn't praise his stories properly, to his way of thinking? He's thin-skinned, you know. And as he says, he may be be appalled morally by her life."

"Maybe he was, Mr. Nathan was, a Jew — we all heard of that, but that's not so bad. I am sure she was not his mistress. Mr. Greeley would never have asked her to write for his paper if she were actually a bad woman!"

Henry smiled at his sister. "I'll put it away for now. We won't mention it to anyone. Let's plan a walk tomorrow — I stored your trousers and hat and the rest of our gear in the shed at the old house. We can go to Fiddler's Swamp and look for pitcher-plants."

Anne married Thomas Bratcher shortly before Christmas. Their cottage occupied the bottom-land of the Bratcher farm's big meadow. In hopes of escaping the damp, Anne set up her easel in the attic, but soon found she had little time for painting. The decorations she painted on the walls of the sitting-room clouded over, in a greenish black mould, during that first wet spring and summer — laughing, she and her husband scrubbed the walls down with lime. She was pregnant then, and laughing suited her. She laughed and sang, and even whistled when she was alone fighting the damp, repeatedly sifting the clotted flour, airing their clothes on the fence whenever the sun came through, and firing up the stove even in the worst heat, to keep the plaster from sagging and crumbling off the walls and ceilings.

She was herself as hot as a stove, an engine of heat, and she stayed strong until her final month, as it happened a very warm September. Thomas built a low seat for her by the spring, with a canvas awning, so she could sit in its shade with her feet in the fine sand of the gently bubbling cold water. There, during her final three weeks, she repaired to weep, gently, for the sorrows of the world. Dolly Allan was dying of summer fever on the lungs and Anne was not allowed to visit the sick-bed. Henry no longer talked to her in the old way or called her Annie. He did not ask her to draw and paint his plant and insect collections, and there was no more talk of Anne making illustrations for Dr. Jaeger's insect encyclopedia. She would never travel anywhere, not to Paris, certainly not to Tahiti. She would be lucky if her life as a farmer's wife would permit her one trip a year to Boston. Her baby might be still-born, or blind; her husband would cease to love her; Sissy or Mother had said something unkind; a runaway slave had been seized in Boston and sent back to the Carolinas to be hanged; the red calf had sickened and died in the night.

She had two daughters in three years' time; and then they waited, anxiously, for a son, who arrived at last, as if the wait had been designed to make his arrival the more joyous, a few years later. By then they had moved into the main house, nicely set up on the hill, with Mother Bratcher, now a widow, and a bachelor uncle. Here the walls were elegantly papered. With her children Anne painted flowers and birds and fanciful landscapes on the furniture — except for the dining-room table and chairs, which Mother Bratcher insisted be left alone. In the nursery, she painted the life-cycle of the tadpole-to-frog around one window frame; around the other, that of the Monarch butterfly, with leaves and eggs on the bottom, three of the gaudy waist-coated caterpillars climbing up the left side, their chrysalides, jade green with dots of gold, decorating the top, and the butterflies taking flight along the right.

In these years, on the rare occasions when she and Henry were alone, Anne sometimes asked about the letter in the desk. Henry answered that it was still there, that no one had come for it or asked after it.

What Henry did not tell his sister was that on one occasion curiosity had successfully tempted him to look at the pages. His excuse was that he had been ill. It had been a cold spring, hardly a leaf in bud in April, and the rain was always mixed with snow. In a very heavy sleet, Henry had gone out to work. He liked the rain, he almost even liked it leaking into his boots, when he waded through pastures that had become ponds, and he loved it pouring off the brim of his hat.

A farmer whose fields abutted Emerson's land in Walden Woods was selling off an additional parcel to the railroad. It was foolish to attempt surveying work in the wet — the steel needles and plates corroded, the plumb lines stretched — but he did it anyway, even knowing he would have to do it again. Henry stood knee-deep in the meadows for two days and then came down with a cough. Teas and broths and bed were his punishment for more than a week, while he lay feverish and dreamy. Once he woke to find the tabby cat stretched out on her back purring beside him. She seemed not the slightest concerned about the Canary-bird, who was chirping so indignantly from her cage in the window that it sounded like yelling. Henry dragged himself over to the bird and threw a cloth over the cage, silencing her, then, faint with the effort, turned back to speak to the cat.

"Oh, Miss Kitty, I feel like the devil."

The tabby sat up and stared at him, cocking her head slightly. The dream he had just left came rushing back to him, so overwhelmingly that he felt dizzy, laid his head down, and muttered aloud, "Margaret!"

The cat bounced off the bed and went straight to the little lap-desk, where it sat pushed against the wall at one end of the big table. With one light jump, she landed on the narrow flat part of the top and, ever so slightly, lashed her tail.

Henry saw, again, Margaret's face — his dream of her talking, animated, at some gathering, then the water, water from the meadows, rising and rising, now a monstrous wave, over her face. He stared at the cat.

Slowly, he shuffled over to the lap-desk, weakly picked it up, and weakly shuffled it back to his bed. He re-made his nest in the quilts, this time sitting upright. He placed the desk on his knees. It smelled of salt and that medicinal tang of sea-weed.

Very gingerly, he tugged back the rickety hasp, lifted the lid, and touched the top page with his hand. Margaret was speaking to him, she wanted him to read this.

He bent over the desk, not taking the pages out, and began to read. He read the first page, then set it beside the pile. He began the second page.

A sense of cold dread filled him and recalled him to reality.

He dropped the page and shut the lid, replaced the hasp, and with more energy than before took the desk back and this time shoved it beneath the table and out of sight. Draped in his quilt, he paced the floor and said aloud, "I'm sorry, that was none of my business, I'm so sorry, please forgive me, it will never happen again."

Reading another person's letter. And from one woman to another. He was, as well as a sneak, a scoundrel. But Margaret would forgive him, and Mrs. Hawthorne would not know.

He never liked having the desk in his room, but felt no temptation to read the letter again. It might as well have been bound with hoops of steel, and guarded by an angel with a fiery sword. Or something like that, fiery swords rising, spinning like spokes of a wheel from the cold under-tow of his dreams.

TWO

IF FOUND, THIS LETTER IS FOR SOPHIA HAWTHORNE IN CONCORD, MASSACHUSETTS. M.F. OSSOLI.

On the 17th of May, 1850, hours out of Livorno, aboard
the merchant ship <u>Elizabeth</u> bound for New York—

My dearest Sophie, as always you are to me—
How extraordinary to be on board & coming home — !
Here I must compose my thoughts. Perhaps I will not send
this to you by post, perhaps one day soon I will sit beside
you on a bench under a maple-tree — how I miss Concord's
maples! — & be able to sit beside you as you read & tell
all that needs to be told. The pages and pages of words I
have offered you & the entire public in print for four years
have been true enough, certainly, & many may have felt that
my partisanship in the cause of the Italian Revolution, &
all revolutions of the people, was not sufficiently measured
or cautious. But if they, if you, only knew to what degree I
was exercising the highest degree of caution, of discretion,

by not telling my private story. Yet still I hesitate. Not from shame, but from something else — a fear of offending, a fear of disturbing the peace of so dear a friend.

— To whom did Jeanne d'Arc confide, when the angels & Mary told her to strap on her armor? & Did these friends weep, or laugh? Surely they tried to prevent her . . . & yet my own reasons, altho' I cannot with that Catholic girl's pious confidence assert they come directly from God, but only more likely that they be the promptings of the Divine within — may seem equally mad, tho' not violent in intention.

What I want to tell you, & you alone my dear, comes from a full heart & an over-full, doubt it not, brain. But I trust that it will unfold, unfold as the pages of this letter unfold, best when you may be sitting quietly — & quite alone, my dear! — when the children have gone to bed & Nathaniel is sitting up in the parlor with his friends, the port & cigars in full fume, & you may scamper to a private attic corner to read.

You are a full-grown lady, by now; you will not <u>scamper</u> up those stairs but rather <u>wend your way</u>. I hope you did not find my earlier letters amiss; I spoke in riddles, perhaps, because I was too afraid to tell anyone the entire truth. (The Entire Truth! As if such a Universe could be told!) But it is all out now — or at least the public face of my life is unveil'd as I return home. Here I am, an old married woman, a Marchesa (such pomp as ill-becomes any democrat but my husband has held to the title for practical reasons) in the bargain, with the best child in all the world & my dear husband beside me. That I did not receive return letters from you did not surprise or worry me unduly; perhaps half of the letters sent to me never arrived because of the war — & because, it must be said, of Italian ways in general. A saying there is: Nothing is urgent in all of Italia but the priest's brandy & the husband's dinner.

There! I am unfair, again, in my old jesting way. The noblest of men, & women, inhabit Italy as well. As you know if you have read my dispatches. Mr Greeley assures me that indeed they were widely read & I believe that this was so. But, despite all my pleas for financial assistance from my countrymen to help the cause of the Italian people, so little was sent.

3 June, Gibraltar

Alas, the journey has not begun well. Our Captain Hasty, a kindly & confident man who had all our trust, has died of the typhus. His good wife Mrs Hasty & I nursed him as he failed — it was a swift but agonized death, & the ship's linen in short supply — and oh! the odors of sickness, again they press on me! — Now we are quarantined at Gibraltar, barely a step away it seems from Livorno. . . . We must wait a few days for more supplies. We will not be able to put his body ashore as he must be buried at sea as a precaution, & this is a great source of distress to Mrs Hasty. Two sailors show signs of typhoid symptoms as well. We are attempting to exercise the same measures of washing & airing that seemed efficacious in the field hospitals in Rome. Also isolating the sick. This is a bad business & I am especially fearful for my husband, my Giovanni, about whom I have yet to tell you in detail — but he was weakened in body & mind from the days of battle — I have begged him to confine himself to the cabin. He, dear fellow, wants to help & so we have agreed he may assist in the galley, making ox-tail broth for the sick. (The cook is also stricken but only slightly.) God willing there may be no more cases.

7 June

We have received our supplies. The cook is well. We think he may not have had the fever at all, but some stray malady that departed quickly. One of the sailors, a hearty Malay fellow called Dark John, has survived. Alas poor redheaded Fredo has died & like the captain's, his body has been slipt, knotted in shrouds, into the sea. The water at Gibraltar is a pale green, with white foam making lace over the surface. It was lovely as well as terribly melancholy to see the white-sail-wrapt bodies fall through that almost celestial green, to be absorbed by that greater Element.

There are no more suspected cases — & as the captain & these two sailors had spent some days together before the voyage in Naples, on an errand for the merchant company — all aboard hope that it was confined to these three alone. Mrs Hasty has become the titular captain under law, but as she is no sailor (& if she were, 'twould make no difference!) the First Mate, Mr Bangs, is at the helm.

We are anchored one more day & then will be off with tomorrow's tide.

The melancholy of the last several days having subsided somewhat, I am pricked with a greater urgency. I intend to tell the story of my heart since last you saw me. My companions on the voyage from New York to London, the Springs, tho' excellent <u>companions</u>, were unlikely <u>chaperones</u> for a grown woman. They were not better informed about England than I — less so in truth in all matters but where to stay & what to eat. Nonetheless they had many friends & ties to assist us in England & on the Continent.

Moreover Mr Greeley felt that the radical step of having his Foreign Correspondent be a woman would be softened if periodically I could refer in my dispatches to my respectable travelling companions. They were sedate enough, heaven knows. My head-aches were extreme in the crossing, & Rebecca Spring was almost too assiduous with the application of balms & words of comfort. & From another good lady on that interminable voyage I learnt quite a lot about the social life to be had in the capital city of Albany should I ever have the misfortune to find myself visiting in that region. I also can recite from memory the receipt for a noxious-sounding comestible, a favorite of a garrulous Carolinian gentleman, called Brunswick Stew, that features squirrel-meat, maize & broad beans.

I thought of you on that crossing, little Sophie — how you were once upon a time the best ministering angel to my headaches. How often to soothe me you would comb and braid my hair, and once I remember you wove apple-blossoms into my tresses. I had reason to think of you again, months later, when I was nursing the wounded in our hospital in Rome — I longed to have the magic of your touch in my own hands, to cure or at least to comfort the agonies of those who died in our care day after day. . . .

But to return to the subject of London. We arrived in August of that year (1846) &, as I dutifully reported to the <u>Tribune</u>, were busy as honey-bees about our sight-seeing, theatre-going, gallery-visiting & high-toned calling on heads of State, both the real (the Lord Mayor! & a member of the Prime Minister's Cabinet who oversees American affairs!) & the <u>soi</u>-<u>disant</u>. The resident London genius, Mr Carlyle, is a stiff-necked man who would have done very well with the stiff-necks of Boston — & I cannot countenance his abiding admiration, nay hero-worship, of that monster Cromwell! No matter how polite I was in print, to you I can call him a Provincial, despite his fame.

His wife is of another breed entirely. She has a bold eye & a quiet step, like a Chippewa brave who would come up behind you with a hatchet in the night. I know she disapproved of me but I quite liked her & can imagine setting her loose on one of our Conversation parties in West Street to mightily great effect.

Mr E warned me months ago that rumors have circulated back home concerning my friendship with Mr Nathan in New York before I left — a lifetime ago now. Some have even said that he & I met up in England, or Munich, to continue our illicit liaison. This is absolutely <u>Untrue</u>. . . . I trust you believe no real ill of me, tho' how the truth gets tangled with the lies in rumor remains a source of wonder to me. I did most sincerely love Mr Nathan — James — with a friendship that exceeded friendship — & hoped, believed, I would marry him. Yet how his being of the Jewish race could so discompose Mr E & others, the very preachers of universal Religion & tolerance — I cannot rightly say. It is harder to live than to preach one's beliefs, I know to my own sorrow. Moreover Mr E has always believed I should remain a virgin vessel, pouring forth the female gospel of the spirit —!

But at the last James Nathan would not marry me & that is the story of it. He meant instead to make a profitable marriage for his business interests, & was at the same time courting me most formally engrossed in the courtship of a proper daughter of Jerusalem, German-born like himself, with a merchant inheritance. (Candor obliges me to add that there was still <u>another</u> young person, homeless & helpless, a girl of the streets whom he had taken under his protection some years earlier — I would have helped her as well, indeed I offered my help when I had learnt by accident of her existence — & I would have endeavored to live with the knowledge of men as they <u>are</u>, had James made it possible.)

When I heard of his planned marriage I suffered the mortification of realising that his intentions towards me were base, that mixed into the gold of our extraordinary friendship there had ever been this dross. Mercifully I had not yielded myself to him utterly by the time he left New York with his dependent in the ship's steerage & his plans for a grand marriage in his coat pocket. Assuredly, I corresponded with him, but I was not following him to London. It is with a continual effort that I refuse to let my knowledge of his character & predilections color my apprehensions of the Semitic peoples as a whole. He would have made me his mistress, like a sultan with a hareem.

& Yet, can I explain, I exulted at the same time I was disgusted, that his esteem for me was <u>as a woman</u>, & that alone. (Sophie, you cannot know what this meant to me. You who were always a pretty little thing, a model of all graces, whose smile I believe was sought by every young man within a hundred miles of Boston, a princess who was finally won by your princely Mr H! . . . To be admired, to be courted, as a woman! James assured me that men of Semitic, & also Mediterranean, blood, can appreciate the stately form & admire the candid face of a strong woman — & this, unlike so many of his other protestations, turned out to be true.)

I recount this foolishness to you, knowing you will forgive me for my moments of vanity & weakness, which were minor. At most my garments were on one occasion disarranged.

Thereafter I demanded a proposal, & received no word for several days; meanwhile an acquaintance, the wife of a clerk at the <u>Tribune</u>, told me about Mr Nathan's other marriage plans. How she knew, I know not; perhaps all the world knew, but I. When confronted, he admitted as much — & then had the audacity to suggest that this should not alter our own relations! What did the man imagine? That I would become a sort of Bohemian mistress, a <u>false</u> <u>wife</u> in the next street while he & his Rachel solemnly raised a family & lit the candles in a house that I, the outcast harlot, might sometimes see by leaning through the palings of a winter night, wishing to warm myself by the sight of their legitimated flames? I am no devotee of silly novels, to countenance myself a romantic heroine doomed to such a Fate as that!

I am angry again, now, to think of it, & at the time did blame myself much, for the freedom of my speech & friendship in the company of such a man that perhaps led him to think me capable of selling my love for a pittance.

No doubt such was the shame I felt, that when Mr Greeley stipulated that I be chaperoned by the worthy Springs, I complied without grumbling. Perhaps I do need chaperones, thought I ruefully. New York, my dear Sophie, is not so safe as Boston for a woman alone. Neither, I can say more happily, is Europe but I mean another kind of safety.

It almost amuses me to speak of this from the great, impossibly great, distance of a few years. So changed am I now; I still see Mr Nathan's behavior as coarse, but I am no longer offended. He is what he is, & should he have ten dozen mistresses, in every Borough & bye-way of the cities of New York & London & Munich, that is no matter to me. I should have taken his measure myself at an earlier moment, ere I lost my heart. Well but I could not have lost it far, since I laid my hands on it again soon enough — a compensating gift of the sea-sickness: when I revived from that ailment of the body, so too did my heart seem restored to me. I was quite myself again by the time we reached England.

Same day, night

The voyage is smooth now; my Nino sleeps. (He is nearly two years old!) At night my husband sits with the men in the rough parlor below decks & plays a kind of Italian patience called "Qui Sace" (Who Knows?), which the Brownings tell me is called in England "The Idle Year." Do you know it? I cannot take an interest in card games, but I see my Giovanni night after night, ever since the war, with his especial deck of cards — these are no ordinary cards but disks with the numerals or faces in the middle & the hearts or spades, the figures, arranged around the circle. These cards have soft tooled-leather backs, reddish, with a figure of a dragon on them. Like so many homely objects I have seen in Italy, they have a charm about them incommensurate with their monetary value, a happy charm of style. Most of them have been so handled that the dragon, black against the red, can scarcely be made out any more.

Giovanni sits for hours, laying out the cards, stacking them backwards into a single pile. He often "makes" the game — because, I believe, he does not truly shuffle the cards.

I run ahead of my tale, again, but I must say how my dear husband is no longer quite the man I married. He was never a man of letters, his English is halting & he cannot read a word of it, but he is withal a graceful & sensitive man with many gentle jests & niceties of manner, a true "swain," whose attentions astonished & gratified me, & with whom I have known a deep, sweetly domestic love. The sadness is that he has been damaged by an injury to his head he received during the last month of the fighting. For a time we feared he would be blind, but his vision has returned only slightly dimmed. His understanding & conversation have narrowed, but how he loves the boy! He can sit with him, playing at tops or cards & cat's-cradle, for hours.

To Tell of London

But now I return to my chronicle & I do promise to be more direct, altho' as you know the shortest distance between two points has never been my particular forte. But back to London with my friends, in the autumn of 1846. Having met Mr Carlyle, & having at last persuaded the Springs to travel on their own to the beauty spots of Canterbury & the southern coast, I had my own time in London. Aside from the constant wish to do well by Mr Greeley's readers, & so to see & hear all that was worth seeing & hearing & knowing in the great Metropolis, I had a powerful desire to walk. & So I did. I found a boot-maker, most of whose customers are constables & messenger-clerks, who made me some very sturdy walking shoes, with a thick sole & brass toe-caps, scarcely different in form from the men's except that in concession to female fashion he added a delicate buckle above the instep. If anyone noticed, I am sure they laughed at me, but I did not care & they were mostly hid underneath the skirts which were, that season, scraping the ground & of course filthy. Never have I had such a comfortable pair of shoes & had I not walked them to pieces in London, Paris, & Rome I would be wearing them still.

Moreover I abandoned my deep-brim bonnets at last. There is a new fashion, "Continental" they call it & not really approved by society but which I have felt free to embrace in my new guise as that singular oddity, the American Woman Journalist — I wear a large squash-cap, something à la renaissance about it, with a flat brim, & a Lisle-veil for occasions when modesty is required.

Women are not allowed in the Houses of Parliament, not even as spectators, which was a sorrow — I had so hoped to catch a glimpse of such as my hero Mr Wilberforce! — tho' I was allowed to watch a trial in the Old Bailey. The pomp of the setting seemed especially sad as it made a contrast to the wretch in the dock who had evidently stabbed his landlord in a haze of drink but who spoke in his own defense by saying that he "loved him like a brother." The wounded man, sitting nearby, was friend & brother no longer & looked away in disgust.

The court wigs lend an antic air. We Colonials who have lived without that decoration for some years & only are acquainted with them from family portraits & newspaper drawings, find them not so much quaint as preposterous. I decided to pretend that I was observing a banquet of the Fi-Ji Islanders all dressed in their ceremonial feathers, instead of the court of law that is our own jurisprudential foundation, & commenced to smile. Human dress is one of my greatest amusements since visiting with the Indian tribes of the Great Lakes & now, since my travels on the Continent. Fashionable rules of dress & decorum, howsoever we act as if they were writ in stone, are so widely diverse & so quickly subject to change that indeed the day may come when you & I, Sophie, decide to follow Madame Sand's example & trot about in Turkish pantaloons. Trot is the wrong word for Mme Sand — she glides. But I am sure that I would at the very least canter in such gear, & flash my brass-toed boots for all to see!

The bridges of London were my great joy. It stirred my soul to walk back & forth across that great River, to see the commerce & the humanity that flowed over & under the bridges. My favorite was Waterloo when I felt I could spare the fee, but I also liked the Westminster Bridge that was Mr Wordsworth's stopping-place for inspiration. He preferred to see London before dawn, while its humanity still slept — "Ships, towers, domes, theatres, & temples lie / Open unto the fields & to the sky, / All bright & glittering in the smokeless air." But I most liked the city when it was awake, the greatest city in the world, with so much that is good & so much that is bad in it, & over all that cloud-strewn sky that glows grey then yellow & pink at sunset. The sky seemed forgiving, a forgiving sea-side sky, offering those "Everlasting Arms" to embrace us promised in the hymn. Somehow to rest in them we must reach upwards — the reaching is hard work, but the final repose is the greater.

Any day in which I felt that I had written accurately about a wrong that may be righted by public action; any day in which I fetched a meal for a beggar-woman & her child or offered my services to a committee that needed me to speak on behalf of a poor-hospital; any day in which I resolved, again, to enter the fray of these times by my pen or by more forceful means — that was a day in which, standing on a London bridge at sunset, I felt that I could view humanity with a full but calm heart, & stand erect to receive the solace of the Divine.

But oh my Sophie, this was not every day! How many days did I lie abed with a head-ache & weep about my failures, my losses, self-regard & self-pity clambering over me like vines upon a tombstone! Even in London I think that I lost one day in five to such defeats & there was one entire week after the Springs came back, that I was obliged by a bad cough to stay in & be nursed.

The day that I came back to health, if not to full strength, we had an invitation to a dinner — it was in November of 1846 — where we met Mazzini, the Italian revolutionary in exile. He was visiting throughout London, hoping to raise money & good will for the <u>causa</u>, for a free, united, & democratic Italy, & having heard of me he wanted me to tell his story for American readers. You can imagine, perhaps, the trepidation with which I approached that first meeting. Mazzini's personal power was said to be great, & like many, I suppose, I was suspicious of the <u>person</u> of a revolutionary, if not his goals. I was prepared to resist dazzlement. I was also, I confess, bracing myself against the smell of garlick & spirits & hair pomade & the insulting freedom of manner that prejudice had taught me to expect of Italians.

Imagine my gratification, to meet a gentleman — at first entirely reserved in manner & courteous — only becoming fiery-eyed when speaking to persuade, standing up from his seat at the table, then raising his eloquent voice — for altho' his English is limited, it has a music in its simple inflexions — gesturing to the small gathering, his voice growing louder as his hands waved more broadly, finally as if he were a very Caesar addressing his legions spread over a hill-side. "My friends in England, my friends from America — my friends who are democrats all! Only a united & free Italy can hope to bring her people into the nineteenth century, to sit at the table with the free men of Europe as I sit here with you tonight! We shall lead Europe again, from the darkness to the light! Too long has Austro-Hungary pressed the foreign boot upon our necks! We are the children of that great legacy of Rome, the model for democracy — an inspiration to our friends in the United States of America & throughout the world. We should claim our inheritance, be the owners of our fields & factories, & in unity bring our suffering, impoverished peoples into the light of progress & reform!"

He was more muted when speaking of the tyranny of the Church — even Italian anti-Papists are all nonetheless devout Catholics — "We have beseeched our Papa in the Vatican to show his support to the people of God, & to suffer the little children to come unto him — to let us turn to him in our struggle. The time may come when he will support our causa. Viva Italia!, & cetera."

It was wonderful drama especially in a London dining-room.

Before many days had past I was urging his cause on everyone I knew in London — some were cold but others made up for that with their enthusiasm. We raised nearly a hundred pounds in a week & a friend of the Springs at the French embassy began to make arrangements for Signor Mazzini to cross the Channel & so head south again secretly as he must through the Continent which did not after all belong to Austria tho' in her pocket. But that might be a year away & so meanwhile Mazzini entrusted me with papers &

a letter to take to his mother in Genoa. We might be some time in travelling to Italy but I agreed, delighted to have a purpose animate my journey more urgent even than writing of the ferment of change to those back home. The Springs would accompany me to Paris & at least as far as Rome. I felt emboldened by the attitude of my new European friends; tho' worried for my comfort, they did not otherwise find it unseemly for a woman to travel alone in their midst. If she were a gentlewoman & had enough money to travel as such, she would be reasonably safe.

Little did I know what would find me in Paris — what I most long & fear to tell —.

16 June, Leaving harbor of Tenerife, Canary Islands
A week has passed. My baby has survived. That is all I can write at present. He caught the fever, he was brave & we almost lost him but we did not. Today he is well enough to eat bread dipped in broth & to walk a few steps. His father never left our side. I am blessed by this love & thank the Divine.

17 June
I write as if from another world. The near loss of my son has made me into a new person it seems. Celesta, the girl who accompanies us & minds Nino for the price of her passage, was sick as well. I nursed her too & became truly fond of her — it is astonishing how waiting for another to breathe,

listening for the air of life, enforces a kind of love upon us. I loved every soldier I nursed in the siege — all but one, who snarled at me like a mad <u>cane</u> until his eyes went flat.

The sailor Tomaso brought me a garland of "everlasting" amaranth flowers & the leaves of that plant, from a Tenerife garden, & they hang where I have tacked them on the upper bunk, just by my head where I sit to write. I have long dreamed of such flowers, since an English lady of my childhood, one whom I idolised, gave me a bouquet to remember her by. Hers were from Madeira, an island just north of us now, that I always longed to see — how close I have come to my childhood dream, by geography's terms! — & how far & how different the life I live from what I could have imagined.

"Madeira" once meant a magical island where I would be fully understood, a place to sail to in my dreams, where love & safety awaited me. Now I know something else — that it is my labor to understand others, & possibly even myself, that will be the accomplishment of my life — the accomplishment in the act of trying. Not to be understood, but to understand; not even, alas, to be loved, but to love.

Nino, whom I love by instinct & yet must still endeavor to love <u>aright</u>, nestles with Celesta now, both of them better but weak, sleeping in the other lower bunk across from my perch. We are so close-wedged that Nino can put his hand on my leg as I prop it across. I almost cannot force my mind to the past —

& Yet, & yet — this near-death, this presence of Death

as real as a hungry wolf in the forest, reminds me of how little time we have — and renews the pressure to tell, the imperative <u>desire</u>. I want to tell the truth, after years of decorous silence —. I repeat that I do not know if I will send this to you. I write to you as if to myself, but with the image of you, as I first saw you with your first child, you the cameo of Motherhood, all forgiveness. There has been much of my behavior that the world would not forgive; I know this. In response to the news of my marriage & child my own Mother has been all sweetness in her letter, but she hints that others will not feel so. Silence from my brothers, confused hauteur from the Greeleys, stern questions from Mr E, & a warm but worried response even from my old friend Caroline — all this has alerted me to the trouble that awaits me, the scornful words & suspicious interpretations. If this is how my friends greet my news, how will the harsher Wide World! It is "worse" than they imagine — & not worse at all as I know myself in this regard, at any rate, guiltless, standing on the axis of the Divinity as pure & true as the day I was born.

———

What is "worse"? I must write of Paris in the winter of 1846–47, & of the great man I met there, the Polish patriot & poet Adam Mickiewicz. I wrote about him in my columns & you no doubt have heard of him but that is not to know the dynamic, thrilling presence of the man, his humor & liveliness, his great soul. I am using the word <u>great</u> often it seems, but as it is one of the only words I can find to fit him it must be his <u>great</u>-<u>coat</u>.

We — the Springs & I — did not meet him until our third month in the city. We spent a full December & January in the heart of Paris life, staying as we were at the Hotel Rougemont, just off the happily named Boulevard des Italiennes. My French tutor was a necessity as I endeavored to catch the <u>nuances</u> of the political landscape in the cafés & on the street-corners & in the salons. Paris enlivened my pen as London had not & I wrote at least six dispatches in that brief time. At last through a letter of introduction to Madame Sand we were invited to meet that extraordinary lady. She had returned from her country home where hunger & rioting for bread had taken hold of the local peasants during a desperate winter — I learned that Mme Sand had given much money & had fed many with her own hands.

18 June

Continuing: On our second visit to Mme Sand's elegant apartment (the color yellow predominated, a fashionable touch), I met the Poet. He is at most times accompanied by an <u>entourage</u> of his admirers & protectors. (I have seen these grown men kiss the Poet's right shoulder as the great man speaks, in homely homage to his sanctity.) I had heard that Mickiewicz no longer writes poems, saving all his inventive powers for the cause of liberty, in Poland & throughout Europe. He has been inspired by the doctrine of Messianism & dreams of the coming of a new golden age, ushered in by Giants who stand tall above the ordinary run of men & women — Poland is a natural breeding-ground for such giants — ah! It can easily sound foolish but as he spoke, it sounded as sincere & simple as a child's prayer, & every bit as truthful. You know that I have long harbored such hopes myself, but here from the Poet I felt as if my hopes had found their proper words at last. I told him of my own faith in the "resurgence," "Risorgimento," & we quickly agreed on the divine inspiration that has brought Mazzini to Italy's cause. It was as if our full apprehension of one another took place in a flash of light, as if no others in the room — including his good friends — were even present. We all spoke in English, out of courtesy to the Springs, but our conversations subsequent to that one were a mixture of French & some German, as well as English, & I learned a few words of Polish — a beautiful language, even when shouted, as there are those <u>shhh</u> & <u>jhhhh</u> sounds, so everything sounds like a whisper, a secret —

. I remember that in that first encounter he took my face between his hands — he is very tall, he stooped over the sopha where I sat, & his hands were so large I felt as if I had been taken into the paws of an enormous gentle Polish bear — a silver bear, as his mane is liberally streak'd with silver — & He said that I was the New Woman, a phrase I had heard before often enough in my travels (do not think me vain, it is how the Europeans tend to speak of American things & people) — But at this moment, I believed he meant also new to <u>him</u> — I was claimed, right there in the midst of the parlor & its inhabitants & its upholsteries — claimed as <u>his</u> "new woman," his enormous grey eyes, that look bigger than other eyes because his face is as broad & stern as a wind-swept sky, telling me — I feared I might convulse from the galvanic <u>shock</u>, I feared others might detect, yet I could not bring myself to remove his hands from my face, dear hands! —

I faintly claimed a <u>migraine</u>, asked for the windows to be opened, & the Springs assisted me home to our hotel.

Rebecca was too careful of my head to provoke me with conversation about our remarkable tea-party, but she did look sideways at me when I said the next morning that I hoped to make another visit to the Poet & his friends. We met him at a private concert that evening — forgive me that, tho' it was M Chopin & he played his own compositions, I remember not a note! — as Mickiewicz gave me a letter, asking to meet me the following day at the home of a friend, in the afternoon. His letter also said what may shock you, Sophie — It said that I did not have the "right" to my virginity, that I needed to know love if I were to be the true New Woman. He had challenged me at first principles — You, who now know me well, know that I maintained the privilege of virginity both sincerely & also, in the depths of my soul, as a solace for my failures with such as Mr Nathan. The Poet destroyed my argument with his words, so bold, so clear — the language with which free men & women must speak to one another, as I believe —

You must not be shocked at what transpired, my dear Sophie — He greeted me at the door, we were alone as I had hoped & perhaps feared. Our first words to one another, even as we embraced, were a solemn vow that we had met & been married in a previous life — we had the same happy notion — he said we had been peasants with a homely farm, I said no, he had been a Roman senator & I his wife — we knew that we had lived outside this time, in the past & in the future — that we were married already somewhere in the Universe —.

& What can be called "good" or "bad" after all? There is only the action that arises from one's true character.

20 June
Cont: The next day I secured a small set of rooms in a side-street near the hotel, belonging to acquaintances who were away from town — & I told the Springs that I needed privacy to write, & nurse my head-aches, during the days. For two miraculous weeks, nearly every day he visited me in the afternoon, as early as he could get away. My rooms were on the second floor; I would slip down to the mews entrance & unlock the back door shortly before he was due — by avoiding the street door we hoped to escape detection — &

he would come to me & stay until dusk. I often called him my "bear," because he was so like a silvery Polish bear, but I also took to calling him, in the style of American slang affection, "Mish." He laughed & exclaimed he had not known I spoke Polish — when I vowed I did not, he explained that the Polish word for "bear" is <u>mis</u>, pronounced <u>mish</u>. & Then he told me that his word for me is <u>ges</u>, said with a honking noise, something like <u>gensch</u>, & that it means "goose."

One thing — & I hope this does not offend — we would, in the calm after the storm of love, set to make one another "spit-&-polish" fine — I in my shift, he in his shirt, would clean & trim one another's nails. I would comb his shaggy mane, clean his ears & neck, snip his stray hairs. He could spend an hour combing my hair — he said it was the color of moonlight. He has terrible scars on his leg & on his head — from when he threw himself from a window years ago, in despair when he had first knew that his wife was incurably mad.

Altho' since he is a man, no doubt he had found ways — he hinted that for some years he kept one of his wife's nurses — what he had longed for were these <u>wifely</u> attentions, these groomings & pettings. I had not known that I longed for them too.

As a matter of fashion as well, he made another great change in my life: No more whale bones! He actually stomped on my corsets with his boots, in a rage that tho' feigned succeeded in "busting-up" the stays. He said it was a garment to which no free woman should submit & urged me to consult Madame Sand about alternatives.

Much to Rebecca's dismay, I did — & discovered that tho' Madame never wears any form of corset herself, she was happy to introduce me to a bandage-like wrapping, with buttons, of softest linen, that resembles something I remember our grandmothers wearing. This old-new soft "corselette" necessitated a lengthy visit to the dressmaker to have all my clothes taken out — Rebecca was appalled — I cannot tell you, dear Sophie, the results! I felt free as a floating angel in my raiment! I cannot imagine that an inch or two more on the waist matters to any but the silliest young girls or the stiffest dowager. (& I will tell you, confidentially, that it matters not a whit to a real man.) Eventually, I had an Italian dressmaker show me how to fashion the loose robes that the women of intellectual & artistic circles in Europe favor, something between a reg'lar dress & a dressing gown, gathered at the bosom, & blessedly, utterly, without stays or hoops.

If Rebecca guessed at my afternoons, she said not a thing. I was so in love that nothing else seemed terribly serious, or fretsome, for a while — never before had I known that feeling of being outside of Time, that attends on two people wholly in love. & Then at last the calendar began to worry me — I received a letter from Mazzini, in which il magnifico urged me to see his mother in Genoa as soon as possible to deliver his letter — but not, he had decided, to try to bring or send anything back for himself, not even through a third party. He had been warned by his friends that, once I visited his mother, my movements would be watched & my correspondence would be read by the authorities. The protection & discretion he had once thought he could secure from my prominence & my rôle as a foreign, nearly official, visitor to Italy, he no longer trusted. Mish at first did not want me even to visit Mazzini's mother, but I reminded him that I was, as he had said himself so many times, "no ordinary woman," & that I did not fear to do what I knew to be right.

All I feared was leaving Mish. He had said, many times, that he must & would sever ties with his wife, but we neither of us, I speak sincerely, believed he should. No matter the terrible things she had done to him & to their children, she was not to blame — only her madness was to blame — & her frailty required his protection. The children lived safely now with an aunt, just outside Paris — how could he be sure to see them often? Moreover, he could not leave France without risking arrest — & If he travelled in disguise that would prevent him from doing his public work on behalf of the great cause.

Our Idyll was broken that day as we discussed Mazzini's letter, & it was made the more difficult because Mish decided to become jealous — I saw him decide, like a naughty boy calculating to throw a fit — of Mazzini, who is not married, & whose letter contained certain endearments addressed to myself. Why must I meet his mother? Why does he call me "his own dear lady" & "his cigno trombetta" (trumpeter swan)? Swan! Ha! I was a goose, but I was his goose, his farmyard goose, &c, &c.

That evening, in the twilight, we lingered longer than usual. We had lost much of the language with which we had begun our courtship, I noticed ruefully — we were no longer the emanations of the Divine, no longer the New Man & the New Woman — but were now only a bear & a goose. He sighed, & said something in Polish. I said, What? He said, "Does God want us in fancy clothes, all dressed up for Church? Or does He want us to come to Him naked as we were born, hair in tangles, tired & scented by the bed-clothes."

Suspecting an allegory, I remained silent. Mish said, I will not say explained, that he had left the priests but not the Church. (He often visited a small Roman church in the lieu, but only when the mass was not being said, & he would leave if a priest spoke to him.)

Did you read any of my dispatches from Paris at this time, dear Sophie? Could you have guessed, amidst my ponderings on the new Europe & my critiques of the paintings, the costumes, the music, & the literature of my host country, that so monumental — & so very ordinary — a love affair was unfolding behind my words?

[blot] What ails this ink? 23 June
I have borrowed an extra dram of ink from the captain's desk, as mine seems to have got stiff from salt. We are in

quiet seas, with a good wind, & all aboard are cheerful since my Nino's recovery is assured. Today he has again been toddling about the deck, like a puppy-dog among the sailors' legs — amazed tho' I am by the speed with which he has regained his health, I nonetheless insisted he lie down for a nap & he sleeps within my sight.

My feet are propped up on a crate of fruit. If we wipe each lemon & orange daily with a dry cloth we can forestall the mould. The smell is heavenly, & I am sucking on an orange as I write.

I come to a difficult part of my story. From Paris we took the stage to Lyons, then a barge down the Rhône — tho' the accommodations were rude, they were not uncomfortable. We then waited a few days in Marseilles (Rebecca had a stomach trouble there) for the packet boat, which we took on its "local" stops along the coast, first to Genoa & then at last to Rome. Rome in April was a miracle of light & joy, I felt I had come home at last & I will not tell of my visit to Mazzini's mother in Genoa except to say that she was a grand & kind creature, & that somehow I think she guessed my secret. My secret was that I was with child, & I had never felt such joy & such fear — a bear cub, to be ours! — (Tho' quickly I tell you, it was <u>not to be</u>.)

We left Rome for the north in late April. Altho' my money was thin, & I had depended on the Springs' great generosity for many of my expenses, I persuaded them to leave me in Venice — they were to travel on to Germany as I would continue my Northern Tour of Italy. — I had written to Mish, I was so terribly anxious to see him & consult as to what we must do — in May I hurried from Milan to Geneva, & thence to Grenoble (oh! the diligences! in the late spring snows!) to meet him within France's borders, as he could not safely leave his adopted country of exile.

Was it the strain of my journey over the Alps? Was it the shock & joy of seeing him again? The new life left me that night, as if my own self were being pumped away from me, soon the hotel bed was a lake of blood, he found me a doctor —.

I mercifully have forgotten much. In two days' time I could walk again. As if I wanted to walk again — I was struck down by the loss of this precious thing — the loss of Motherhood itself it seemed, & this fruit of our love. I was wrung dry of love, of hope, indeed of all feeling. I thought God had left me, that I was a fallen woman. For the first & only time I wondered if I was being punished for my sins. (Oh, but in time I realized it was not a punishment — something more complicated — not a blessing, but perhaps a preparation?)

I shall never forget the day of our parting — Mish sad, almost stupefied by his sadness, holding my hand as we sat on a cold bench in a little park, Jardin de Quelque'chose — I remember the names of nothing from Grenoble, I rejoice that I will never see that horrible town again.

For some time we talked, almost idly, of the Divine. I told him how dear George Ripley had enlarged my thinking years ago when he insisted that the Revealed Truth of the Gospels does not require a belief in the miraculous & that all of the events of Christ's life may be explained by science. Mish was indignant in defense of miracles.

Very gently, I told him of a man I had just met in Rome — a young man, Ossoli, of good family, of his republican sympathies, of his kindness. Of what the Springs & all who had met him thought of his character & his sincerity in his addresses to me.

Mish said, "It is as I imagined for you — as I hoped. Since we cannot continue — this is what I would have wished. If he is worthy, only if he is worthy."

"You give me away so easily, then?"

"Not easily but I will not lie — it is a relief, to know that you will be cared for. He has money? He will help you continue your work?"

"He admires me, but he cannot read a word of English. He — it is odd, it is perhaps the Italian way — he seems almost to <u>worship</u> me, as he would the Madonna or his own mother."

"Ah. Then you must never tell him."

How did I continue on my travels, & continue to work, after this parting? What tears & what dismal future I saw, all my golden dream of life with my Great Polish Bear sunk in a pit of tar.

I will never know how it is that the human body can continue, a soldier answering the winded horn of Necessity, tho' the spirit has lain down to die.

& Yet within a week or two it was as Mish had predicted — travelling throughout the north of Italy without a chaperone, I spoke more to the people, my conversation improved, I was the American Lady, or more often if inaccurately, the Inglese, an oddity & nonetheless a personage, wherever I went. I made many a friend in the villages & cities, strangers eager to talk to me & feed me & offer me a room for the night with their families — laughing or solemn, as their education had prepared them, at the sight of a copy of my American newspaper. I think it was stranger to them that I was an American & a journalist than that I was a woman. The city sophisticates I met included Horace Greenough & Madame Arconati, the Storys, the painter Hicks & alia.

By October, I was ready to return to Rome, to see again my new ardent friend there, & to make a new chapter in my life.

I cannot write any more. I will see if my Nino is awake & take him up on deck for fresh air.

24 June

Always, always money! The men are arguing about their pay, who gets what share if the marble we carry is sold at such a price, who deserves what, who is working harder, what the late captain promised — ! My poor husband, frightened by loud talk, by anything loud, retires to the cabin to brood. He is in the bunk behind me as I write — not asleep, but perfectly still & curled up like a mouse under the rug.

Nino is with the cook, & Mrs Hasty keeps them both in hand. It appears that Celesta is growing fond of one of the Italian sailors.

A History of My Life's Economies

I am born in 1810, the eldest of nine children, in Cambridge, Massachusetts. My ancestors are a muddle of Tories & Colonial Rebels, agitatingly always in politics as well as business & farming. My father, Timothy Fuller, was so eager never to shrink from a fight that he was known to start them with no provocation whatsoever. His marriage to my mother was a love match. It was not economically expedient, as he was a politically ambitious lawyer & she came from an altogether humbler & quieter family, the Cranes. His eventual rise to State Senator & then to Representative to the Congress of the United States cost more than these positions paid into the family coffers tho' he continued his legal practice.

My little sister Julia's death in 1814 (she was 2 years of age) was an emotional <u>expense</u>. I was not aware of things in terms of cost at the time. Life has been eager to educate me in such economies since. As the number of children grew, we occupied a large house in Cambridgeport & when Father went to Washington for many months of the year we lived comfortably but also sparingly. In winter Mother set our beds around the chimney at night, explaining that even sticks of wood & coals were costly so we must warm one another.

I read everything. Father had trained me from the age of 3 to read English, Greek, & Latin. Later I acquired German, Italian, French, Hebrew. I read Schiller & understood the words long before I understood the meaning. I had head-aches from the age of 5 & occasional convulsions from the age of 13 tho' my health never impeded my studies if I remembered to take air & vigorous long walks.

At the age of 9 years I am sent to day classes at the Port School. It costs $12 for the term. I show some improvement in penmanship under the writing master, Mr Gould. From him I learn that ink from the shop is a luxury but that we can mix our own with linseed oil, chimney soot & pine spirits.

At the age of 11 I am sent to live with a family friend in Boston & attend Dr Park's School during the week. I take top honors & do not make friends. This costs $15 for a term. I also attend dancing school, twice a week, $1 a week.

For reasons perhaps related to the cost, Father removes me from the school at Christmas & brings me home to live with Mother. In a make-shift school-room in the back parlor, I begin to teach my brothers & my sister Ellen how to read & write. At 13, I accompany Mother to my first afternoon parties. I seem to remember that two new dresses were required for each season. I do not remember the exact numbers, but estimate each dress made by a dressmaker for hire is nearly $5. Those we make at home cost considerably less. I am clever with my hands & become the family seam-stress tho' Mother is unhappy when I make myself a dress of crimson satin which she says is unsuitable for my age. When Father comes home from Washington he forbids me to wear it in company.

In 1824 I am sent to board at Groton School in the country. For some reason I never hear the cost. It is possible that Father traded my education expenses for some political or family favor once shown the owner, Miss Prescott, as this school is in the town where Father grew up & knows everyone. In 1826, Father buys a grand "palace" on Dana Street in Cambridge. The President & Mrs John Quincy Adams come to dinner.

The baby of the family, Eddie, dies in my arms from a fever in September of 1829.

By 1831, Father's political career is unsteady but he says that his legal practice still clears him $20 a day. Nevertheless he decides to retire & become a gentleman farmer; he sells the Dana Street house for $8,000. As the family is temporarily homeless, I am sent to live with my Uncle Abraham in his Brattle House, a mansion-cage. I have a mystical vision of the All & resolve to forget the self & selfishness. It is clear that I will need to earn money to support the family now.

Father buys a 28-acre farm in Groton. It costs too much (I never know exactly how much) & will require the employment of himself, his wife, & his now 7 children to make it prosper. I do all the sewing & work in the dairy with Mother & we save school costs by my teaching Ellen & my brothers. I look for work translating in the hopes of earning extra money.

Upon Father's death, in 1836, we learn that the estate is worth nearly $20,000 but that most of it is tied up in the land. Mother cannot continue to run the farm by herself but with the boys & with two tenants to help, she can get by. Once the Uncles sort it all out, my portion is less than $1,500, not even enough to finance a trip I had hoped to take with friends to Europe. (I was going by a calculation offered by a knowledgeable friend, that it would cost $5 a day, with an additional "cushion" of $500 for unforeseen expenses.)

At the advice of Harriet Martineau, whom I have met through my Boston friends, I embark on a biography of Goethe. It is around this time that I first meet you, my little friend! & All your wonderful Peabody clan: Your fine mother & sisters & dozens of friends as well. Meanwhile, I have taken courage from the example of your sister Elizabeth, who hosts "Conversations" in Boston, lecture-classes for ladies, for which she charges $15 a "series" or "term." By moving to Boston & living with an aunt, & with Elizabeth's kind tutelage, I am able to do the same. With a combination of German tutoring & Conversation classes I acquire 25 students! About half my income I send home to Mother. Through the help of Elizabeth & of Mr Emerson, I am able to sell three literary reviews to Boston magazines. ($9!) I am "launched."

At the same time, Mr Alcott opens his Temple School in the upper floors of a Masonic Temple in Boston. I teach languages there in the mornings — and my other job is to record as secretary Mr Alcott's own "Conversations on the Gospels" with the young students. It becomes clear after the first few days that for prudence's sake I need to stop writing down what he says & what the children reply. He is a large-minded man but he seems to have a knack for making trouble.

He does, in spite of my discretion; students are withdrawn & the school is shut down after one year. I am offered another teaching post, in Providence, at the handsome annual salary of $1,000 but hope I need not take it. I certainly can support myself on my private pupils & am eager to make progress on my Goethe biography. Alas in the Greater World finances crumble; I see my first "economic slough," & Mother & the boys need my money if they are to be tutored & go on to College. I take the job at the Greene Street School in Providence.

Boarding with the mother of a colleague & teaching in Providence, I am in exile. Providence might as well be Borneo. Letters from Mr E, Caroline, & a few other friends are my sustenance. I teach Latin, composition, elocution, natural history, ethics & the New Testament to 60 pupils. (Twice the 30 I was originally promised.) I try to celebrate my exile by taking advantage of solitude: In the evenings I work on my life of Goethe & on a translation of Eckmann's <u>Conversations With Goethe</u>, which I hope to sell to a Boston publisher.

I am privately convinced that the Uncles are preventing

Mother from selling the farm — if she did she could move back to Cambridge, which she would prefer. Also the sale of the farm would free my brothers to earn their own money for their studies. The Uncles say that the economic crisis of the country forbids the sale of the farm. Meanwhile they make threats to Mother that they will take her boys away & send them to live with wealthy relatives. I write to her that I will never let this happen.

In August, when I am on vacation from teaching, I spend some days in Concord with the Emersons; on August 31, 1837, I hear his Phi Beta Kappa Address, our "intellectual Declaration of Independence," in the First Parish Church of Cambridge. I discover that, by virtue of my association with Mr E, Mr Alcott, & others, I along with they have been dubbed "Transcendentalists" in the journals. This term of derogation (suggesting as it does a denial of Christian principles) shocks both enemies & friends sufficiently that my dear companion Caroline, who was to have come to Providence with me for the winter term to study at the school as a special student, is prevented by her parents from so doing.

This is both a personal & an economic blow as I was to have received $28 for her tutelage.

Uncle Abraham releases some funds from the estate to allow schooling only for Arthur & Lloyd in the fall. My sister Ellen comes to me in Providence to study with me privately, & Mother visits me as well. We are only a little crowded in my one room as I spend most of my day at the school. Meanwhile I embark on teaching weekly evening classes in German. This money is all for Mother.

29 June (or is it 30?)
I have lost the thread these several days. Sea-sickness, mild for me & more pronounced in the cases of Mrs Hasty & my husband. In the last two days the winds righted themselves & all felt better, but by then it had become imperative we address the matter of the lice. Mrs Hasty & I set up a sheep-shearing station & cut the hair of all the men who would allow it, close to the scalp, & then we greased everyone with pork fat. Poor little Nino cried at the smell — it was fierce — & Then Mrs Hasty & Celesta & I combed & greased one another's long hair & braided the tresses & pinned them up. Two days having passed, with the aid of the cook's stove we set up our station again, this time to wash away the grease — along with the dead lice & their eggs — from our heads, & the bed-linens, all! Two more days for this chore! & An extra set of sails strung across the decks! It is to be hoped we shall not have to go through this tedious & smelly exercise again this voyage. I am not sure the men would agree to it again in any case.

30 June
No longer scratching, I return to my financial reckoning:
    A gift of friendship & a savings of summer expenses! In 1838, the Emersons invite me to spend my three summer

months with them in Concord. I cannot say enough about the recuperation I experience in these blissful months, free from immediate money troubles & solaced at all times by the friendship, instruction, & conversation of Mr E. Since Henry Thoreau is never far from their house himself (working as handy-man for the house-hold & general poetic interlocutor for Mr E) I get to know him well; he has an independent philosophy about Economy that he tested by two years of living in a cabin, scratching beans from the field & pulling fish from the pond.

Come the fall, our family finances are worsening. My brother Eugene has had to leave law school. Only Arthur, enrolled at preparatory school in Waltham, can be educated this year outside the home. Mother at last is able to sell the Groton farm. I sell two Goethe poems in translation. Total income from poems, my own & in translation, thus far: $3.50.

Things are very confusing in these months: I become exhausted by teaching, I leave the school at the end of a year & a half. I go home to Groton (where the farm is sold but the family may stay on for a few months) & work on my Eckmann translation, finally giving it to my publisher, Mr George Ripley, with a long essay on Goethe's work & life — this is the last I ever see of my "biography," alas! — as a preface. The book is praised, my essay is lauded, but it never sells well enough to repay the publishing costs & I do not see, as they say, "one thin dime" for all my labors.

April, 1839: Mother & the family are settled into a large but modest house in Jamaica Plain, five miles or so from the center of Cambridge, where Mother plans to take in boarders. The Emersons ask me to live with them through the summer. Relief from the immediate need to earn money is a great balm; my health is again restored in the Concord woods & fields.

& It is this summer that I first try a vegetary diet, hoping at one & the same time to train my body for higher thought & to learn to save income (in the future, when I am not a guest at a sumptuous board) by not eating meat. Henry Thoreau tells me about roasting a wood-chuck & eating the meat half-raw, I think to see if I will scream but instead I solemnly quote from the <u>Georgics</u>, where Virgil sings of the gifts of the earth, "Munera verstra cano. . ." & Henry smiles sweetly as one defeated.

Mr E thinks I am wrong-headed & mightily fulminates against my "Hindoo" practices, but Lidian joins me in the vegetary regimen for nearly a month & claims to feel freer in her mind. We both "lapse" together & laugh at our newly voracious appetite for fowl, ham, &c, but I had mastered a salutary lesson in surviving on beans & corn & greens & fruit should the time come again when it would be expedient or necessary.

July the 1st
Cont: I am quite entertained by this "autobiography in dollars & cents" tho' I will probably spare you some of these

pages dear Sophia. Soon we will return to the "autobiography of the heart" on which I initially embarked.

Quickly, then: When I left Concord to live with Mother at the end of the summer, I hatched a project with Elizabeth who would sponsor my Conversations — as you well know who were in most faithful attendance. (Had you met your princely Mr Hawthorne yet? I cannot recall.) My Conversations support me for some months in the winter & spring of 1839–1840. My first series earned me $200, & I doubled the price for the second series so was now earning nearly what my Providence salary had paid. The cost to me was an invariable head-ache, enough to fell me for two days afterwards; but I kept the work going for five years & had over 200 students during that time.

Meanwhile Mr E had offered me the editor's post at <u>The Dial</u>, where I began work in 1840. Subscriptions sold at $3. Contributors were paid so little that I ended up writing most of the copy myself for some issues. I was paid nothing & I never labored harder at anything, before or since. (& Some money, & my as yet only dimly seen future, arrived through this as well: I wrote "The Great Lawsuit: Man versus Men, Woman versus Women," that Mr Greeley of the <u>Tribune</u> offered to publish as a book, <u>Woman in the Nineteenth Century</u> — & which, when it came out at last in 1846, went into editions world-wide with seven translations, became my calling-card everywhere I went in Europe . . . & from which I earned the only money I ever made from a book thus far — $85!)

The summer of 1843 I took a long trip to the Great Lakes with friends & wrote the book <u>Summer on the Lakes</u>, which eventually was published but from which, again, I earned no dividends.

By the end of 1844 I was finished with the Conversations & done with the <u>Dial</u>, which struggled along for a year after I left it & then collapsed in obedience to the market-place tho' Mr E swore he did not lose more money by it than he could afford. Mr Greeley pressed me to come to New York & write for his <u>Tribune</u> with an offer so tempting — as it seemed to me — to write essays on literature, the theatre, the conditions of women & the poor, reporting or thoughtful, as I liked — to write 250 articles, at $5 each, in a year — & to save much that I earned by living as a guest in his home, a "country" farm in Turtle Bay only a few miles north of the city. $1, 250 for a year's work! A princely sum!

Oh what a year ensued. To earn my salary & write an article nearly every day, in a house-hold where I was chastised for my personal habits, including & most importantly, drinking tea! The Greeleys had long since given up eating meat — & I was glad of my ability to be abstemious in this regard — but they also, on the grounds of both health & spirit, forbade themselves a host of other foodstuffs, including fish, tea, coffee, sherry, honey, white sugar, eggs, cucumbers, & pepper & nutmeg. I rebelled to the extent of insisting on my tea & also kept a private stock of honey & eggs in my room. I was more sociable than I might otherwise have been in that year, angling by the rushing stream of society for any invitation to dine that might come my way, sometimes at James Nathan's hotel, & was able thereby to get a substantial meal perhaps one day a week. It was during this year that Mother told me she no longer needed my reg'lar remittances, as the older boys were able to pitch in & with Ellen's help she was able to keep boarders in the Jamaica Plain house.

One more financial note from this time: When Mr Nathan departed for Europe, he entrusted to my keeping his enormous Newfoundland dog, Josy. She promptly killed two chickens belonging to the Greeleys' neighbor (thereby interrupting my egg-supply & requiring my out-of-pocket replacement of the fowl), so I employed their boy to feed the dog. Her enormous appetite required such a quantity of horse-meat & grain-mast that the whole cost me nearly $2 a week! When at last my urgent query when Mr Nathan would return to reclaim his Josy was answered by him with the suggestion that I turn her loose because animals can fend for themselves, you may imagine that what little regard I had left for Mr Nathan's heart was crumbled into dust.

Happily Josy was soon placed with a prosperous family which boasted three romping little girls, at a country estate up the river.

Another thing I learned at this time: Discretion can be expensive tho' candor costs more. Discretion costs at most such trifles as the hire of a hansom & a slight sense of shame;

candor costs the earth. The Greeleys knew nearly nothing of my friendship with Mr Nathan & moreover I felt it wise not to speak of my frequent dining with any friends, as the first such occasion resulted in a quizzing such as you cannot imagine, as to what exactly I had eaten — with such a hand-wringing about the duck, & the berry-sauce & the joint & the peppered turnips, the cakes & creams, & the claret — !

My obligation of writing copy for the <u>Tribune</u> cost me some friendships in that time. Caroline, & Mr E, & a dozen or more of my dearest correspondents could not understand that I no longer had the leisure to pour forth my thoughts privately on the page, as all such thoughts were now claimed by the public sphere. Well I felt from Up North the cold mutterings that I had become a frivolous city scribbler & had succumbed to the vulgar blandishments of the market-place.

Perhaps because I never felt any diminution of your regard, dear Sophie — perhaps because so much of what we felt for one another was wordless — & was simply, as the poet Herbert has written of an even deeper connexion, "something understood" — that I cherish our friendship through all that has happened in these years. I see your dear face, silently listening as Elizabeth & I talked into the early morning. I feel your hand in mine as I guided you along the river path when you were with child. & I remember how often, in those first months of your marriage, when Nathaniel would take me on one arm & you on the other, &

we three would sally forth into the Concord evening — how I loved you both, & loved your love for one another!

I must not be distracted by sentimental tears; my tale of dollars is nearly done. I had told everyone I knew that I wished to go to Europe. Mr Greeley, tho' unable he said to pay my expenses, would be interested in commissioning me to write regularly for the <u>Tribune</u>. Marcus & Rebecca Spring proposed themselves as my saviors & companions, as they had a plan to bring their young son to be educated in England for a year while they visited the Continent. They would pay my passage to England if I would consent to tutor their boy on the voyage to prepare him for the rigors of an English school. With what I had saved & sums from a range of friends & a small advance from Mr Greeley with a promise to pay twice the rate he had paid me before — $10 a column! — I was able to amass my supply of $2,000 & so we embarked.

Alas there has not been a moment in the last four years in which money was far from my mind. Mr Greeley paid me but not always quickly & once the Springs had left me on my own in Italy I was bereft of my accountant Marcus & his habit of advancing me funds until money from New York arrived. For the first time I needed to apply to Mother for help, & from time to time as well my brothers, Mr E, & other old friends sent a "donation" to the "cause" of my bed & board. For many weeks in Rome I kept an "economies" note-book in which I entered every purchase, as dear Henry Thoreau taught me once — & by eating only bread & fruit,

& allowing friends to buy me coffee, I was able to live on less than one dollar a day, including rent. Fortunately I was often taken into the homes of people we met for dinner & during the siege itself most everyone shared what little was to be had. (Twice I used my payments from Mr Greeley just to buy hospital supplies.)

My husband's family had land & property once upon a time & while Giovanni's father was still alive he had some small income. The Ossoli family are of the "Papal Aristocracy," so his two elder brothers, following the family tradition of Vatican service, were soldiers of the Papal Guard. Giovanni, with his much older sister (more like a mama to him since his own mother's early death), had stayed at home to care for their long-ill & lingering father. The anger in the family when Giovanni joined the Civil Guard & spoke with revolutionary fervor! I met him when he had just done so, & his father had for a time forbidden him his presence.

Unlike many others in the Democratic, Unitary, Associationist, & Revolutionary movements (& these are only 4 of the many shades of the causes of the people & not always in accord amongst themselves), Giovanni was never fooled by the Pope's words — he believed, as was shown to be right by later events, that the Pope would turn against our Revolution at last. But it is curious. He who has in his quiet way raged most persuasively against the betrayals of Pius IX cannot bear for others, such as Protestant Americans like myself, to criticize the Holy Father even now. I am grateful that he cannot read English because he would be angry at what I have written in my book.

Now I am well & truly done with the sordid account of My Life in Economies.

3 July

Cruel irony! I write of my tea-drinking at the Greeleys & my supply of tea is stolen. My head aches & I cannot write today. I suspect a midshipman named Cole.

Later, same day

The men have pooled what tea they can spare & brought me more than I lost. Once I had restored my spirits with a strong brew, I gave a speech of thanks where many of the men were gathered & there was some laughter & some tears as for all the best speeches ever given in this world tho' my eloquence was not the cause on this occasion but rather their generous & tender hearts.

4 July

Mr Bangs fires a salute in honor of Independence Day & we Americans on board (I believe there are five of us all told) sing "Yankee Doodle" as the colors are flown. Nino cheers along with the pip-pip-hurrah! I have made a small flag — from a square of white canvas, red ribbons & a scrap of blue flannel — & to Nino's delight have sewn this badge onto the front of his jacket, over his heart.

I have also promised the men a recitation this evening &
am trying out several texts to see what I remember best. Mrs
Hasty would appreciate a rouser such as "Once more unto
the breach" but I cannot bring myself to celebrate even so
noble a king on this day. Am trying to remember the third
verse of Mr E's "Concord Hymn." On this green bank, by
this soft stream / We set today a votive stone / That something something may redeem. . . .

7 July
Head-aches & small discouragements — Celesta has been
weeping about her sailor & there are bruises on her arms
where he has handled her roughly. Nino lost his spinning-
top overboard & wept. I heard one of the sailors refer to me
as the "Signora vecchia," the "old lady," so in preference to
weeping I stared myself out of countenance in the looking-
glass. It seems my hair is as much silver as it is golden, &
lustreless. There are shadows beneath my eyes & the flesh
of my jaw & neck in repose hangs like a curtain. I fear the
return home, I fear old friends as well thinking me an old
lady, my years of force spent by motherhood & the suffer-
ings of the body & the pietàs that were our daily lot during
the siege.

Does not America chafe under the tyranny of her young?
Well we might contrast the respect — nay more than that, the
reverence — that is shown in Europe for the elders, male &
female alike. Mme Sand is older than I nonetheless she is the

axis round which an entire world spins. Grand-parents are the center of every social gathering they attend, not bundled off to a warm corner & ignored as they are in America. Is it because the country itself is so young, & so dependent on the energies & the new ideas of the young, that America begins to despise its old folks? & Even calls them "old folks," instead of "Madame," or "Signor," or "Sir"?

Well since I am coming home, will-I-nill-I, I must prepare myself to feel & act young again & so keep pace with this American necessity. Heaven knows I wish to <u>act</u>.

8 July

Now the time has come, my dear, to tell of how I came to be the married lady you will meet in a few weeks.

As I already explained, I had met Giovanni Angelo Ossoli in Rome in early April of 1847. He escorted me home when I lost my way after vespers in St. Peter's, & took to calling on me at the rooms we had taken on the Corso. Later in Grenoble, I told Mish all about him — & then by letter Mish continued to urge me to take the step of marriage & said that he prayed I might experience the joy of motherhood at last. I was so grateful. I had lost my "beloved" but I had not lost the Poet himself; my beloved had become like my father, advising & urging me to do what would make me happy & fulfill my place in the world.

It is no insult to the Poet to say that he like all men perforce under-estimated the cost to my physical self that becoming a mother would mean. No doubt he also imagined, as indeed I did, that having a husband would mean I would be protected & could continue in my work. But as I am now circumstanced, with a small child & a war-scarred husband to support, how am I to take "my place in the world"? This is a puzzle I am yet working out, one that I hope my friends in America will not refuse to help me solve. I hope that Mr E will not gloat that he was right, that solitude & chastity & barrenness were the requisite conditions for me to be the New Woman & raise my beacon of education & action aloft. Minerva & her chaste moon are all very well for school-girls to emulate. But what World worth its salt will deny women the creature necessities of love & motherhood as the price for participation in its decisions & its future? The Associationists, I believe, have many practical solutions to offer, with their plans for community nurseries & schools. . . .

But there are times when I long only for this: That my husband & child would venture on an excursion for a few days & leave me to my solitude. Would I write a newspaper column? A chapter? No. A letter begging for money from an old friend who is feeling less friendly with every letter he receives? No! Would I mount a platform & urge the rights of slaves not to be slaves, the rights of a free Europe, the rights of women? Not I. I would sit with Goethe's poems, & attempt a translation. I would take a walk, a long city walk in which I could day-dream amidst the throng, their dreams & mine twining into the thick rope that is humanity . . . I would stand on a dock & watch the boats, I would dream in color & music but not in words . . . & then I would return to my desk, make a pot of tea, & try to make the German words come alive in English before me. This I would do for several days until I felt like <u>myself</u> once again.

———

Upon our reunion in Rome that autumn — October, 1847 — Giovanni pressed me to marry him. His father was ill, & we could marry as soon as his father was dead. (This sounds a harsh calculation — but think. I was not a suitable wife, an American & not a Catholic; his father was already furious that his youngest son was an impious revolutionary & the additional shock of marriage to such a one as I might end forever his family ties & his hopes of rightful inheritance.) Such was our case, & still his father lingered in this life, & the earthquake of the coming Revolution was beginning to rumble beneath our feet — bread riots in the countryside again in France — Vienna in an uproar for a constitution — the Austrian General Radetsky building new fortifications in Milan because the people had gone on strike, refusing to buy the tobacco & pay the taxes that fed the Austrian army, & rioting in the streets. Naples was in turmoil. Rome was shaking with energy & anger & we believed the Pope would take our part.

Imagine my feelings, if you can. Giovanni, this dear man,

whose presence was both a delight & a comfort to me, who showed me so many graceful yet manly courtesies — at any moment he would be fighting & he could die. We did what I believe any people of true feeling would have done: We stood, just we two, in the Lady Chapel of the Santa Maria Maggiore, before Giovanni's favorite painting of the Virgin. (The "Virgin of the People," as she is rightly called. Can I describe adequately the tenderness of her gaze, the archaic stained gold dappling over the surface of that ikon which reminds the petitioner before her of the centuries of hopes & fears she has met & allayed?) We joined our hands, & whispered to the assembled saints, the stone floors & the rafters of that church, our vows. We were truly married then, & so my own date of marriage is November the 8th of 1847.

We found that I was with child in January. I was also so ill from my condition & from the dark Roman winter that we hardly knew if I would survive. Before any chance of reconcilement, Giovanni's father died in February. Much as he had hoped that his sister would have say over the disposition of the estate (as their father had pledged she would) alas his eldest brother took all legal control & refused to listen to her pleas for the rights of Giovanni. The brother was if anything more angry than the father had been about Giovanni's revolutionary ideals & immediately besought the magistrate for a writ to prevent my husband from claiming his inheritance. By April, we were confidently hopeful that the baby would live — & indeed my health began to improve with the coming of the spring, & with news of the Viennese "republic," & then of Austria's routing from Milan, & our spirits soared. This being the case, & anxious to secure our child's future rights, we were officially married (before a priest, & filing a paper at the local registrar) on April 4, 1848. But for the time my husband felt that maintaining secrecy was still essential. Ever hopeful that all would come right with the estate, he was anxious not to add this news as fuel to the fire of his brother's wrath. Thus our dilemma: desirous of being above-board & honest, but doomed to secrecy — temporary so we believed! — so as to protect our love & our child's future.

Public events soon overtook us all — tho' as the horses of change plunged forward no progress was made on the estate's disposition. Giovanni had always expected to inherit a small farm & modestly prosperous vine-yard his family owned in the Tuscan hills north of Rome — such he had always believed would be his maintenance & support! How he agonized in fear he would lose it! How painful it was for me to keep all this a secret from friends back home! With every week that went by without telling you & all my family & friends, the difficulty of telling & the fear of not being understood grew worse. Yet was I joyful. The gestation of a new Italy & my new Child became as one in my mind in those months.

Mickiewicz was able to cross the border to come to Italy! Austria, internally in disarray & weakened at its northern

Italian garrisons, could no longer enforce its standing arrest warrant against "dangerous" Polish nationals. First he gathered a group of Poles from various cities in Italy, received a blessing from the Pope, & then they marched as a battalion into Milan with a banner proclaiming the rights of all men, civil rights for Jews & for women! While his men stayed behind to hold the line against the Austrians, in May he came to Rome!

I had heard that he was near, I sent a note by <u>guardia</u> courier to tell him where to find "La Signora Ossoli" & for three days & more I quivered listening for his step on the stair. Then on the fourth day: It was just before dusk; Giovanni was not due home for a time. The door to the street was not locked during the day, as many tenants came & went, & whenever that door was pushed open, the wind in the vestibule rushed up the stairs to the second floor where I lived, making a little "whooshing" sound at my door, like an unearthly knock. I heard it; it was he, I knew. As in the old days, awaiting his approach I felt as one suspended in air, my head & heart floating in those seconds as his heavy tread, slightly uneven like a heartbeat, came up the narrow steps. I opened the door so he could see me whole before he spoke — he placed his hands where my child was sleeping inside me & kissed me as the tears wet his face.

"I am glad!" he said.

Then Giovanni came home & as we had agreed asked Mish to be our child's godfather.

All right; I hear your objections: Reason dictates that we must take this scene in hand. What? you exclaim: A woman with child, with her husband & her lover both at her side, & they all at supper? How can this be? Even in a French novel of the most scandalous & progressive sort, surely at the least the woman, & probably both the men as well, should fall a-wailing at this juncture, & threats of duel or suicide should be all that tongue can utter?

Reason & dramatic decorum must topple together however, when I tell you that on the contrary we laughed & toasted our friendship & that Mish was all kindness & Giovanni all goodness & I the happiest of women. For the nonce at least. Did Giovanni guess at the past that Mish & I shared? I think he believed the Poet & I had a rare friend-ship & I know he was, & is, too great of soul himself to be jealous of that.

So it is that the next generation forms our lives & we conform to theirs. Our sole duty, rejoicing in the lives to come, is to make the world better fit for them, on our hearth-stones & in the broad world.

My husband & the Poet also had their faith to share & next day we three went to hear the mass together, Mish for once tolerating the presence of the priests. Giovanni had decided in his quiet way that as I was in my heart & soul a Roman woman, so I was for all purposes a Catholic. I never quarrelled about this as we were I believe trusting in the same Divine being. When, much later, our marriage became known & friends in Italy wondered at the "mixed" nature of our alliance, Giovanni always silenced them with a simple, "No, Margherita is also of our faith" & I think he believed that he had converted me with his love & our original marriage vows before the Virgin.

10 July, Very calm seas, pleasant on deck but sails flat
Today I must take myself in hand & resolve not to become impatient with Giovanni. His nightmares have been keeping us awake & he whimpers like a baby all night. I cannot have two babies, I tell him unkindly, but I am trying to remind him of his courage & his manhood. The man who held the Pincio Hill in the midst of the siege, day following day, to fire the last cannon at the French, who led the ragged last bits of the army to fight until they dropped around him — this man weeps in my arms & moans like a second Nino every night. I am grateful he cannot fully understand the hurtful things I sometimes say to him — tho' I know my harsh tone flings barbs that catch in his heart.

I am very tired, & in danger of <u>despair</u>, the only mortal sin I believe in & fear.

11 July, <u>Wind</u>! Brisk & homewards
Returning to May of 1848: After a few hectic weeks, during which I sat for my portrait — Mr Thos Hicks was very insistent that it be done & tho' I was heavily robed I was uneasy that his anatomist's eye would guess my secret — in

early June I left Rome for the mountains north & east of the city — first at Aquila, later in the Apennines at Rieti — to spend the last months before the birth in peace & privacy. What feeble explanation did I make in the <u>Tribune</u> for leaving Rome just as her Revolution was at hand? My health, & an interest in the customs of the peasantry, I believe. I wish that I could say all was well as I waited for the new life within me. But tho' I found servants, I was never able to pay them enough to guarantee loyalty. For a certainty they none of them believed I was as poor as I said — their experience with ladies of the <u>Inglese</u> variety was not vast but it had taught them to expect ample reward for service. In Aquila I found a saintly older woman who wanted to mother me & would have done so for no money at all; but I needed to be closer to the city & to Giovanni, & so moved to Rieti — where I was met with sloth & insolence by the servants Maria & Guidetta & their family of spongers.

Was ever a woman waiting for her first-born in such a state as I? I wondered aloud in self-pity, only to be answered in an instant by common sense: Yes to be sure, the world over, now & throughout history, women have had to endure worse than this as the world tumbled & rose about them. I thought often of the stoical Indian women I had met at the Lakes — how they endured poverty & childbirth without comment (or, to be accurate, any comment I could <u>make out</u>). I was daily anxious for news of my husband, as the streets of Rome were filled with demonstrations, some peaceful & others not — the Pope having turned to Austria for help at last in a betrayal whose immensity we could hardly credit, so the Civil Guard was in skirmish with the Papal Guard, & the Duke of Naples sent troops to disperse the crowds. I was much relieved when in July Giovanni left the city to recruit men from the countryside. The farmers, as always except in times of drought, were traditionalists & resistant to the call for change. & Yet Giovanni was a persuasive leader — something about his quiet & truly aristocratic demeanor, combined with his simple words & passionate eyes, compelled many men from the villages & towns to follow him.

Indeed how simple — through all the turmoil of politics, the complexities of alliances, the daunting imaginary architectures of future states — remains the basic claim: That men are equal in the eyes of the Divine, that the worldly power of some individual men does not give them the right to torment, oppress & deprive their fellows; & that the powerless many, if they unite, can be powerful against the few.

Meanwhile I was experiencing an interesting & no doubt ultimately instructive loss of personal power, there in the village of Rieti. The goat I had purchased for too many lire, so as to have milk every day, was taken from me by Maria's mother — to give milk to her loutish son who was a hulking 12 years of age & would have been better served by a switch to get him to work. Oh no, they explained when I demanded the goat's return — I had only <u>leased</u> the goat

— that payment was by the week! So I paid & paid again. The goat herself was white, dappled with brown, & had a large purple wen on the side of her neck. She fed on the grass & thistles & her milk was delicious. Alas, she chewed through her tether every few days or so & we all spent much time chasing her, tho' I was now not much able to scramble about the hills & sometimes despaired that the family, so misnamed Cherubimi, would never find her again.

Thus was my final month — August. I was too hot & too ill to work. I had no home for my baby, no nest for my little bird, only the make-shift of hired quarters & squabbling attendants. My feet had swollen so that only rush-weave slippers fitted me. My teeth ached, often so violently that they woke me in the night. Tho' we were well up in the hills & so should have been safe from the <u>malaria</u> that plagues the Roman summer, the air was heavy & the nights were clogged with the damp & with biting flies. The good Dr Carlos bled me twice which strengthened me & I believe forestalled the convulsions I had sensed coming on. He had guessed that my age was greater than I allowed — (I was 38, tho' my husband believed I was but 30, such is my vanity) — & he feared for the life of his foolish <u>Inglese</u> patient & her unborn child.

Perhaps my age was the reason, or that same dark fear that I would again be punished for my sins, but in my heart I did not fully believe that I would survive this ordeal. I dreamed constantly of disaster, fires & floods & walls falling on me.

Perhaps the reason I had agreed to sit for Mr Hicks was that I wanted some memento to leave my friends — it did not seem possible, most of the time, that I or my baby would live.

By the middle of August the wicked Austrian Redetsky had pushed through Ferrara & headed for Rome. The first news made me scream with fear — for my husband, for Mazzini, for all the men & even for us here in Rieti — Dr Carlos gave me a sedative drink so that I could sleep a little. It was days before we received word that the battles were stalled & a stasis, a <u>stand</u>-<u>off</u>, held once more.

& It was Dr Carlos who helped me place a bench & a broad green umbrella beside a little spring that bubbled from the hill-side just below the old well. Even in the high heat of the day, & aided by the thin shade of an olive-tree, the umbrella allowed me to sit for an hour or so with my feet in the cold waters & so find some relief, & some numbing of my fears.

13 July, Strong wind

The lice have returned <u>con spirito</u> but there is no way to address the plague in this windy weather. Poor Nino cannot stop scratching his head to runnels of blood — so I have again salved him, this time trying a mixture of lye with the pork-fat as Tomaso advised. Mrs Hasty disagrees & says it will burn & meanwhile Nino is crying so I cannot think straight.

Later. Following his third head-washing, Nino sleeps in his father's arms. The lye did scorch his scalp & I am sick at my

foolish mistake that pained him so. The smell in the cabin —
it can scarcely be called a cabin, let us call it a cupboard — is
ferocious. I press a lemon to my nose with my left hand as I
write, holding the paper in place with my elbow.

Giovanni arrived in Rieti in time for our son's birth on
September 5th. I cannot remember all — that there was
pain & that I suffered I do not deny but Nature seems intent
to give us the blessing of forgetfulness. (It is the same with
all the mothers I have spoken to, but one —. She claimed to
remember every throe, but then — she is a friend of Mme
Arconati & from time to time a soprano at La Scala.) Some
day very soon I will ask for your own insights about motherhood, my darling Sophia.

Angelo Eugene Philip Ossoli. <u>Tanto</u> <u>belo</u>, my little one,
my Nino! Amidst all my fears for his life & mine, I did not
dare think ahead to the great love that would arrive like a
thunder-clap! I swear the heavens themselves broke open
when I gave birth & the cooling rains came to Rieti like the
blessings I suddenly knew.

A month & a little more — I had milk fever & could
not nurse — the perfidious Guidetta refused to nurse my
baby, a desperate day when we thought he would die from
hunger. Then we found the lovely Chiara, another of the
far-flung Cherubimi-Seraphimi clan, who came to us &
fed him amply — strange quiet days marked by intervals
of sleep & holding my baby, as the autumn rains gently fell
& the grass & leaves on the hills turned first green again,

then golden & then brown. I would crush a grape & drip the juice into Nino's mouth — it was like feeding a little bird. Even in his first days he knew me & turned his face to me wherever I was in the room, & only would rest quietly when in my arms.

Into the serenity of the nursery, however, the world's tendrils crept. One such vine was the war itself — as the rest of Europe lost her nerve, it seemed that it remained to our Italia to lead the way to a new world, as our Revolutionists gathered strength & hope. Another vine that wound about me, now that I believed I would live & Nino would as well — was the necessity of money. Again & again, money. My secrecy about my circumstances had led those at home to be mistrustful, & perhaps those who might have helped with gifts & loans were hesitant. Also — I learned that many believed I had come into an income when my Uncle Abraham had died, indeed I received two letters congratulating me on my good fortune — such congratulations being baseless, as I received nothing whatsoever from him, in punishment no doubt for my years of taking Mother's part. A great-aunt's promised gift on her death was likewise a disappointment — instead of her estate, some $50,000 which she willed to her church, she left me her books, all still in Boston, & $100, which went to pay for food & the doctor & Chiara & so helped save my son's life in the moment, & for which I am grateful still, but otherwise did not rescue us. I had privately lost all hope of Giovanni's inheritance — at least until after the war, & then who knew what the new world would offer. All our hopes must be pinned to my book, which I had begun in the spring & worked on in the summer as long as my health would permit — my "History of the Italian Revolution." Writing that would require much time & effort & moreover — moreover — I must be back in Rome to witness the unfolding of the history I was to write.

Letters having got lost & misdirected across the ocean, Mr Greeley was impatient that I had not written for him since June. When I got his late letters, in November, I saw that he offered me a raise — $12.50 a column! — if I would only write more. Obviously, I must return to Rome immediately.

Chiara had a relative she could board with in Rome & we began to plan a move in November. But Giovanni would not allow it, firm as he was in his belief that all would come right with the family inheritance & so continuing to hold to our policy of secrecy. Already we had paid Guidetta to keep quiet — she often asked for more, & we gave her what we could spare. Unlike her cousin, Chiara was no <u>black-mailer</u> but she was simple & a talker & our baby's presence in Rome could never be kept discreet. Alas, alas — I left Nino with her in Rieti. My very bones ached, as Giovanni held me in his arms & the cart jostled us the 40 miles or so into the city, 40 miles between me & my darling, 'neath the drizzly November sky.

14 July

Mother-love, so fierce, like a magnifying-glass held over the tinder to make a forest fire!

15 July, Sea choppy

Celesta & I have managed to air the cabin & its sorry linens. Husband & baby sick, Mrs Hasty also, but all now asleep. The sailor Tomaso has given me a small rope-bracelet with wooden beads that press against my wrist — a salt's remedy or charm against sea-sickness that aids me immeasurably.

Mr Bangs says that a storm is behind us & will whisk us north & east & home in a matter of a day or two. I had best speed my pen as well.

My story now is in the winter of 1848–49, & into the spring, the months of the Risorgimento, the Roman Republic & then the terrible siege. Oh, to recall the thrill of those few months of Rome's freedom — the Pope having left in November! (I liked to pretend he left because I returned, but in truth he left because he was a coward & feared assassination.) The Assembly in session & daily new declarations & new laws passed for our freedoms! Freedom of the press! 250,000 Romans casting votes in their first elections! The Inquisition declared illegal & its monstrous building shut down! Many wanted to burn it but cooler heads prevailed — as fortunately cool heads prevailed throughout that halcyon time — to propose that the building instead be made into new homes for the poor, or perhaps an asylum for orphans. Mazzini came in & out of Rome, for he was wanted in the fighting in the Piedmont & then in Naples — every time he came into the city, he paid me a visit in my new rooms on the Piazza Barbieri. He was tired but hopeful — & like my Giovanni, like all the men, seemed to have derived some super-human strength in those glory days of freedom. Daily we prayed for expected help — money or arms from England, & at the very least diplomatic recognition from everyone's beloved America.

During these months I was able to visit Rieti for two weeks, in April. The family was quarrelsome & rude, I worried about the cold, as the cottage there had only the one fire-place in the kitchen, but Nino's cradle was always on the hearth & all seemed well. After two weeks in my arms & bed, he cried when I left but was soon comforted again by Chiara & so the agony of leaving was chiefly mine.

As I had long predicted, the return of the conservatives in France meant that instead of offering salvation, as some had once fondly hoped, France as enemy sent ships & a full battalion to restore the Pope to "his" State — landing on the coast at the end of April & laying violent siege to Rome & its brave people for many terrible weeks. Cannons fired all day long into the city. The Princess Belogioso, with admirable efficiency, organized field hospitals. I was delegated to run the one on Tiber Island called Fate Bene Fratelli.

Early on, a boy with a wounded leg had the gangrene setting in — the one doctor for five of our hospitals was not around, who knew when he would return, not that day or the next surely — we had no surgery saw, & so I asked one of the only men who was able — his own head-wound had nearly healed — to fetch an axe, & while I & another woman held the boy's arms he chopped off the leg just below the knee. It took three whacks, & as the boy did not swoon at once I was obliged to sit on his chest to keep him down. Then I sat by & pressed the bandage all night to make sure the bleeding stopped, until in the morning the doctor's boy arrived with his bucket of hot tar & we were able to sear the stump. The soldier did survive — unlike so many others — & lived to hop about on a wooden peg. But tho' he called me Mama, as all the boys & even most of the older men did as well, when in distress — I felt like no Mama I had ever wished to be.

Many of the children of Rome had been sent to the countryside, but some orphans & others, less fortunate, came to the hospitals for safety & we made use of them to fetch & carry & fed them what we could. We also enlisted the prostitutes, who worked nobly & without rest. We tied red armbands on the women & children to mark them as helpers & to them all I was also "Mama," or the "Signora D'oro," for my hair.

Mazzini held the city for longer than anyone had thought possible. The ancient walls held, & barricades went up in the streets. French troops sometimes breached a wall, & there would be a skirmish in the Vatican gardens or at the Quirinal, but the aggressors took many losses & were always beaten back. The difficulty for us was that no one outside came to our aid, not even with food — all the Catholic world was in an uproar of indignation about the ousting of the Pope & allies we might have hoped for in England or America, even from Norway, did not see this as a fight that they would join.

It was during this time that I became convinced that the institution of slavery in the United States had so weakened the moral fibre of my countrymen & women that they had lost the will to fight for freedom abroad — even when such freedom was in the spirit of our own articulated Constitution & vision of the rights of man. & So the pernicious effects of slavery extended well beyond my own country's borders.

& Slowly, as with any siege, those trapped within began to flag. I had moved to rooms in a quiet corner in the north-east of the city; but soon the fighting was visible from my windows there as well — I saw close up to my eyes the guns & blades & men bleeding in the streets, like some ghastly <u>Carnevale</u>. The noise day & night was terrible, the unholy blast of gunpowder, the scraping & crashing of metal & stone & I sometimes left my bed to sleep on a cot in the relative quiet of the hospital, where the groans of the wounded & dying were at least human.

In a battle in the Borghese Gardens, Giovanni was

wounded in the head & lost his vision for two days. But at the end he would not leave his exposed post on the Pincio Hill, through all the cannonades of the end of June — Except to visit me on one fateful night, June the 30th. He had not slept or eaten for days. I fed him & he dozed for some few minutes. I begged him not to go back, but he said that he would & I believed as if with a premonition that he would die — I followed him against his will, I said that if he would go, so would I. I hoped to make him fear for my life & so not go — or fear for our boy should we both die — perhaps I wanted to die too, as all seemed hopeless & the sound of guns & blasts in one's ears for days & nights, the bracing of the body for the sound in the brief silences, jarred the sense from one's mind — If he would go, then so would I, I said, & followed him up the hill as blasts sounded close by — .

The hospital wagon had just passed, collecting the wounded, nevertheless by habit I reached to touch each body to make sure the soldier was not still alive. There were more dead men than I had seen in one place before — perhaps 40 scattered over a quarter-acre of ground. Rubble of pavilions, benches, & old pathways, trees snapped in two or uprooted — it was like some terrible giant had grown tired of his toy-town & in a tantrum had smashed the whole world. Some bodies were so torn apart that there was no mouth or nose on which I could lay my hand to feel for breath. The air was a yellow cloud of powder-fumes.

As we drew close to my husband's post, where a group

of men sat & lay together in a heap, the noises suddenly stopped.

I felt dizzy, as if the silence itself had struck me.

Or it was as if, stepping onto the crest of the Hill, we had stepped onto a stage & that was the <u>cue</u> for the sound to cease. At the very moment when we both might well have died, the cease-fire was begun.

Mazzini, who never would surrender, had surrendered. We had lost.

Later, & again later still, I shook as with an ague with the realization that I might have orphaned our boy that night. I cannot explain it — except to say that all the boys fighting & dying were my sons & my husband was my son & then I ran out of mother-love & wanted at last to die myself.

It was not a <u>frame</u> <u>of</u> <u>mind</u> likely to visit one in anything less than such circumstances. Please do not think me a coward if I say that tho' I hope for revolutions again wherever the tyrants oppress the people, with equal force I pray I shall not myself be called to battle ever again.

Same day, later

Ocean again serene & I have endeavored to wash our soiled linens. (I do not believe Mr Bangs knows much about the weather or what to expect. We now fear we will not be home for a week more.)

& Yet I must contradict myself. Tho' I trust it will not come to war, as surely it will not, I am prepared for the battles in

the newspapers, in the legislature, & on the streets, for the
great cause that awaits me at home — what is also your own
cause, I am sure, of Abolition. Which must & will be mine
as well. (Your sister Elizabeth was one of the first I heard
speak passionately & publicly on the subject — I can still
remember the welcome shock of her insistence on the words
"our African sisters"!) America needs to be a bright beacon
of hope for all the world, undimmed by the shadow of her
historical crime of slavery — together we will make it right
and I am ready for that fight surely.

All but two of the fruits are too mouldy to eat, & these,
along with some maggoty rye-meal past eating even by the
goat, we have tossed to the fishes.

16 July
Where is our promised wind? We are off the Carolinas
now, not in sight of shore, but the ocean carries smells of
the land — a real, green smell of trees in the wind, & vastly
many more birds. Impatience is our companion. I see her as
she might allegorically be represented, a woman in tattered
clothes wringing her hands & with wild eyes fixing her gaze
at the horizon — but hold! Impatience is none other than I
myself.

17 July, Wind
I will be fretful & complain a little about the events of this
past year. We staggered away from Rome, almost ashamed

but withal grateful that by surrendering Mazzini had ensured that Roman lives would be spared by the victorious French. We had almost no money, my husband's brother had taken over the vine-yard he had hoped would be his own & his last illusions of any inheritance dissipated into the air.

& When we arrived in Rieti to fetch Nino he was nearly dead from starvation. The erstwhile-beloved Chiara had shown her true family colors — with a new child of her own to nurse, she had been feeding my baby on nothing but wine-soaked bread, I knew not for how long! It was the only time in my life when I have struck another person — that family hearth, so often the scene of vulgar quarrels, must have brought it out in me. I slapped Chiara's face & to tell the truth punched her, until restrained by Giovanni & I believe I might have strangled her, so hot & complete was my rage & so intent was I on her ugly screaming throat & mouth. Her baby wailed, contributing to the scene an additional music of squalor. Fortunately the doctor — not my good Dr Carlos, who had joined a cadre of troops, but some other — arrived & managed to calm everyone with sedatives & reassurances.

My own little goat was gone, but the now loudly repentant family gave us another nanny-goat for milking & we loaded up the cart & headed for Florence, where Madame Arconati had found us rooms & where we could settle while I finished writing my book. The journey was extraordinarily terrible except that within a day or two it was evident that Nino would thrive. How he loved the goat's milk!

DEAR SOPHIE, THE SHIP [BLOT] IF [BLOT] TOW [BLOT] PRAY MY NINO [BLOT] NOT FRIGHT [BLOT]. 18 JU [BLOT] LO [BLOT] M.

THREE

Shreds of thick tea-colored paper still stuck to the wood inside the lap-desk. Anne scraped gently at these with a fingernail, releasing an old smell of iodine and salt. She rubbed at the scratches on the steel lock and hasp she had pried off with a small file. The stack of pages she held on her lap, like a creature. Would she read them? She still could not decide. It was early on a September morning in 1882; it had been more than thirty years since Henry had first shown her this letter, when they had wondered how to deliver it to Mrs. Hawthorne. How unearthly the feeling — like the whisper of the sea in one's ear, a sound one almost ceases to notice over time but of a sudden with meaning articulated, the sea itself trying to speak in sentences, now that she had at last seen these pages again. The longer she did not read them, the more difficult the prospect of reading them seemed.

She needed to take a walk. She tucked the pages back into the desk, but left the lid open. Rummaging in the back hall for her boots and hat, she stepped on the collie-dog's paw and in the agitation of his yelping stepped back abruptly and banged her head on a coat peg.

"It's nothing," she answered Mattie, her servant, who had stirred and called out from her room next to the kitchen. "I'm fine — go back to sleep." She was almost disappointed, gingerly touching her scalp, to see there was no blood.

As she pulled on her boots, the dog whined his excitement and she remembered Miss Fuller's words: "Complete. A complete life of its kind."

The meadow was heavy-soaked with dew, waiting for its final cutting of the season, and she had to drag herself through the high wet grass, tangled with vetch and bedstraw, to get to the path by the creek. The damp clung to her skirts and she wished again that she could still wear trousers as she had when she was a girl, secretly, when she went adventuring with Henry. The dog chose his stick and she threw it, again and again, into the water.

It was in the spring of 1862, when they were learning of the terrible losses at Shiloh, that Henry died at last from consumption. For three years he had been an invalid, and in those years Sissy had scarcely left his side.

Anne's husband came home from the war in 1864; a month later he died of puncture wounds in his stomach that would not heal. Their son, not much more than a child at his father's death, had taken over the work of the farm with two cousins. He went on to buy and sell land and had set himself up at last in a prosperous coal-and-kerosene business in Boston. Her daughters had married — the younger, who had long been a trial to her mother, moody and difficult, had gone west with her husband; the elder with her husband and five children still lived close by in Lexington.

Most of the Bratcher acres had been sold off at considerable profit. A mill and gravel works was now in operation a mile down the creek, the woods had been cleared and a dozen houses clustered there, a peach orchard had been attempted and abandoned, the dairy had closed, and the richest land still was given to vegetable crops and hay but farmed by a man who was a tenant.

When she was not making her visits to her son in Boston or her daughter in Lexington, or having them and her grandchildren to stay during the summer, Anne lived alone with a woman servant and a handy-man in the old homestead, set up on its knoll with a small barn for the horses and a fenced yard. She had never travelled far; her son had long promised her a jaunt to New York City, but when he and his family had gone there for a month last spring, there was no mention of her accompanying them. Sometimes she tried to interest her friends and children in a summer trip to Cape Cod, but nothing had come of that either and she was reluctant to go alone. She did take the train into Boston a few times a year, to look at paintings and go to lectures and concerts with friends, and she must be content with that.

At his death Henry had left Miss Fuller's desk along with his specimens to Anne — although their sister Sissy, fierce guardian of his papers, had not permitted her to take immediate possession. With their parents both gone, and after Sissy's death in 1876, Anne had quietly collected the desk and the specimens from the house-hold of furniture before the heir, a cousin of their father's, moved in. The desk had been refitted with a new steel hasp and lock; she guessed that, at soon Sissy had understood the papers were not Henry's own, she had locked them up and set them aside.

In the six years since Anne had claimed the desk it had sat on the floor in a corner, under the jumble of things in her work-room. This was formerly the dining-room of the Bratcher homestead, now set up with her easel and paints along with articulated wooden hands and heads; printed model landscape figures of alps, ruined towers, windmills, church spires, ice-bergs, and the like for copying; assorted urns and plaster fruits and dried flowers for her *nature-mortes*. Those specimens of Henry's that had survived the decades — a dried wasps' nest, a hundred shells, many seed-pods, a full wood-chuck skeleton, a fox's skull, and Indian arrow-heads, belts, and baskets — covered the shelves, side-board, and fire-place mantel throughout the room. The Canary-bird they had once rescued was stuffed and perched, along with three New England song-birds, on a piece of birch-wood in a tall glass bell jar. Sometimes she used these objects in her paintings as well, as emblems held by the subject in a portrait, or on a window-sill in the foreground that opened onto an imaginary landscape.

She did not sell her paintings; those friends who indulged her by sitting received a painting from her as thanks, but she knew not to inquire too closely about whether or not they hung the trophy someplace more prominent than the spare bed-room or the attic. No one had ever offered to pay her for a painting. She still had problems with perspective, but now and then she pleased herself by an illusion of depth. One of her own favorites was a painting with the Canary-bird sitting on the window-sill, the window open and in the distance, an assortment of people, a picnic party laden with baskets and blankets, climbing towards the viewer from the bottom of a yellow and green meadow. Her daughter, loyally, said it reminded her of a painting by Mr. Inness.

A curious incident in that summer of 1882 had prompted her to think of Miss Fuller again. A friend sent her a book with a note — "You knew the <u>dramatis</u> <u>personae</u>, did you not? I hope this will amuse you." The book, newly published in London, was called *Day-Dreams of the Utopists: The Transcendentalists and Their Legacy* by J. M. Rushworth, described in the preface as "An American Statesman and Home-Spun Philosopher from Virginia." Rushworth mocked Emerson as the "grand old ostrich of Concord with his head forever in the sand," "ignorant of the plain facts of God, commerce and human nature," a "preacher of the gospel of Himself." Anne guessed that Mr. Emerson's death that year had occasioned the book, or perhaps emboldened the press to publish it. The late Mr. Alcott was similarly derided; Mr. Channing, still alive, was barely cited. Though dead, Henry was spared; he was mentioned only as the "half-Red Indian, half-Stoic versifier and shadow of Emerson." Attacks on William Garrison and Horace Mann — not Transcendentalists at all of course — suggested that the author was chiefly writing a political tract against the Yankee notions of Unitarianism, liberal education, and Abolition, though in the current climate he was not brave or fool enough to attack Abolition directly.

It was in the chapter on Miss Fuller that Mr. Rushworth's style of invective became most pronounced. She was described as "myopic and a hunch-back," physically ruined by a father who had forced her to study "like a Medieval scholastick," love-sick for Emerson *and* Alcott, a "self-declared Sibyl" with "strings of gullible girls and overgrown boys at her feet," whose *Woman in the Nineteenth Century* was "long-discredited," who had written "Socialistic propaganda on behalf of the Italian assassins in the pages of the *Tribune*." She had disgraced her family and friends by a romance with a German Jew in New York, then by "falling into the embrace of the Papacy" in an unproved marriage with "an Italian so-called nobleman, one Ossoli," who had "been duped into rescuing her from the scandal of her liaison with Mazzini," and who was "most certainly not the father" of her "imbecile, and possibly mulatto, child." Anne learned that Nathaniel Hawthorne had lampooned Miss Fuller in his novel *The Blithedale Romance*, published two years after her death, where she had appeared as a snake-necked sex-goddess of destruction named Zenobia. (Rushworth explained that the historic Zenobia, for whom the character was named, was a fourth-century empress in Palmyra who murdered her husband and child.) Rushworth described the Ossolis' deaths as "tragic but mercifully swift."

The chapter ended with an anecdote about Miss Fuller visiting Carlyle in London in 1846. "She approached the great man with a pronouncement: 'Mr. Carlyle, I am ready to accept the Universe.' 'By Gad, woman, you had better!' he replied."

Wondering a little about laws of libel — *could* one libel the dead? — Anne of course thought of the desk and its letter. She recalled that she had learned of Mr. Hawthorne's death several years ago, but was Mrs. Hawthorne still alive? Wouldn't her sister Sissy have taken care of that detail, assuming she had noticed to whom the letter was addressed?

Anne wrote to an old family friend, the Reverend James Freeman Clarke, at his Boston church. Did he know if Sophia Peabody Hawthorne was alive and where she lived? Mr. Clarke's reply arrived: Mrs. Hawthorne had died, more than five years ago, in London. He was delighted to hear from Anne, he said; and could he be of further assistance in her inquiries? She sensed she had pricked his curiosity; but instinctively she did not wish to confide in him. Feeling brave and a little reckless, she wrote instead that she was simply widening her education, and asked if he would write her a letter of introduction so that she might use the library at Harvard.

In September, Anne ventured into Cambridge on the train. The sound of a bell boomed the hour as she entered the Harvard Yard. Flocks of gowned young men burst from the doorways and swirled about under the trees, jostling her and then apologising with exaggerated courtesy. She threaded her way through more men up the steps to Gore Hall. At the front desk she handed over Mr. Clarke's letter for the inspection of a gloved attendant; he rang a bell and murmured to a much less elegantly dressed fellow with a clerk's swaddled coat-sleeves, who fetched another just like him. Flanked by these two, she was ushered past a card catalogue, where worked what looked like a dozen women in aprons, to the Reading Room. At a table in an alcove, under the amused, or simply curious, or even outraged eyes of many men, young and old, she spent the afternoon. The librarians whispered suggestions and retrieved items. Carefully she looked into books — the two volumes of the *Memoirs of Margaret Fuller Ossoli* (selections of Fuller's writings, with essays by Emerson and others), a posthumous edition of *Woman in the Nineteenth Century,* a collection of the *Tribune* columns from Europe. She noticed from the fly-leaves that none of these had ever been borrowed from the library by any Harvard students. She had brought a note-book and short pencil that fitted into her reticule — with these she took notes without being sure what would be helpful. She wrote down: *No one reads her work. Memoirs: Ed. by Emerson, Clarke, Greeley, Channing. Henry quoted but did not contribute. Emerson quotes Carlyle as saying that MF had "a high-soaring, clear, enthusiastic soul."*

One of the librarians brought her a sharper pencil.

To page through the old newspapers and journals, bound in great flat green and black leather boards, like atlases, she had to stand up and lean over the table. She saw, on the front pages of the *Tribune* from the 1840s, that Miss Fuller's account of the events of the Italian revolution ran down the right-hand column, and that she was often paired with another *Tribune* correspondent, the German writer Karl Marx, whose columns ran next to hers. Both wrote about the war: Miss Fuller from Rome, about day-to-day events; Mr. Marx from various other European capitals, where he reported on what others thought of the war and something he referred to as "the international workers' struggle."

As well as contemporary reviews of *Woman in the Nineteenth Century*, she also found some lines that mocked Miss Fuller, in a longer work in verse called "A Fable for Critics," by James Russell Lowell. It had been published while Fuller was in Europe. In a firm set-down, Lowell said that she stole the ideas of others, that she was spiteful, and that she wrote with "an I-turn-the-crank-of-the-Universe air." Anne tried to remember where she had seen Lowell's name already — ah, yes, in that article by Miss Fuller called "American Literature: Its Position in the Present Time, and Prospects for the Future."

Her back ached from leaning over the table. She asked one of the librarians to find Fuller's original article, and after some time he returned. She resumed her stance. It had been in the *Tribune*. Oh. Well. Miss Fuller sounded as if she had every right to her opinions. She sounded very learned, in fact. And not at all spiteful — generous, rather, and hopeful even for work she did not like. Ah — here was James Russell Lowell's name, alongside Henry Wadsworth Longfellow's. Miss Fuller decidedly did not think that the future of a new American poetry lay in their hands; Longfellow parroted the works of others, and Lowell was, she wrote, "absolutely wanting in the true spirit and tone of poetry."

Anne put a little note in her book: *She made everybody angry.*

Bewildered by the size of her task, she leafed through bound copies of *The Dial* magazine; half of its pages seemed to have been written by Miss Fuller. In her note-book, she listed some subjects: *American Painters; New Poetry; Poverty; the American Indians of the North-West.*

She read accounts of the ship-wreck, several obituary

notes, and the essays and reviews that accompanied the publication of the *Memoirs*. In Boston the writers were kind; in New York and farther afield, they were less so. She knew she was not imagining it: Here was that same feeling she had been surprised by so many years ago, when Miss Fuller had died. Everyone was — *relieved*. Not actually glad that she was dead, perhaps. But surely relieved, relieved of the burden of this impossible woman. Relieved that they no longer would have to read her exhortations to do good, to send money, to think more broadly, to consider the poor and the powerless, to worry over their place in history, to follow her difficult sentences, to wonder if women after all should be allowed to pester them in this way, and to do such things as Miss Fuller did and imagined.

She made everybody angry. Such a terrible talent.

Flanked closely by two ushers to the door, as if she were a horse that might rear in traffic, Anne stepped out into a misty evening. As she had been reading, the world had been transformed into softness and muddle, and the eye was drawn to small patches of clarity where the gas-lamps lit the paths. How could one reclaim the private person one had known, even if only a little, in the midst of the clamor and eloquence of public opinion and reminiscence? She concentrated very hard on her own few memories; she summoned up her own words. Under the lamp-light at the Yard gate, she wrote in her note-book: *More alive than anyone else.* And then: *She frightens me.*

The day following her Harvard visit Anne drove her pony-cart to the public library in Concord, to borrow *The Blithedale Romance*, the novel of Hawthorne's she had learned was supposed to be about Miss Fuller. Not much of a novel reader as a rule, she struggled at first to understand what was fantasy, what was allegory — since clearly the narrator was meant to be a figure for Hawthorne himself, and Blithedale was like Brook Farm, in Roxbury, where Hawthorne had briefly joined his many friends in the early 1840s to run a communal farm on noble principles. (She remembered Henry's muted horror at the scheme — or perhaps just at the very idea of living with that particular company — and remembered also that Miss Fuller had not joined them either, as she was too busy elsewhere.) The very disclaimer from the author at the start of the book was, Anne surmised, a kind of code: I'll say this is *not* Brook Farm, that these characters are *not* based on figures from real life, and by my so saying you will understand the reverse. Anne could not make out who the powerful, sinister Westervelt and Hollingsworth were meant to be exactly — the Reverend George Ripley, who founded Brook Farm? Mr. E? Alcott? — but she was pretty sure that the feeble and pretty Priscilla was a sort of Sophia Peabody (loved by the narrator) and that Zenobia, despite her "dark" hair, was Miss Fuller.

Named for that powerful queen of ancient history, Zenobia of Palmyra, who murdered her husband and son, this

Zenobia of Hawthorne's imagination was beautiful and mesmeric, rich and richly dressed, preaching a doctrine of female emancipation although she herself longed only for a man's love, hiding an illicit marriage, enchanting the narrator and Priscilla and everyone around her — and then bringing destruction, mostly upon herself. She committed suicide by drowning at the end of the novel.

Anne pondered these things, and returned to her notes to write:

> *Mr. H. wrote the novel soon after MF died; and it is filled with love and hate. He is unjust in his portrayal of her as idly rich, as she surely was not. He also believed his wife, "Priscilla," was in her power. Did he suspect Sapphic tendencies? (Good heavens.) Do novelists do this often, kill a person a second time? Would he have been happier if Miss F had committed suicide? Did he somehow imagine she had? But how can a ship-wreck be suicide? Does he suggest by giving her the name "Zenobia" that she murdered her husband and son? Did he confuse her power with the power of the weather itself? The goddess of hurricanes.*

In any case, thought Anne, Miss Fuller had certainly occupied Hawthorne's imagination.

At last, not sure if she should, less sure of everything than she had been even before her researches began, the next morning, at dawn, almost as if she were ceremoniously opening a tomb of the Pharaohs, she took a file and broke open the desk lock. The interior still smelled, sharply, of the sea. She touched a button, a drawing-pin, three tiny buds dried on a knobbly stem — she recognized the plant, *Amaranthus graecizans*, or was it *virids*? — a clam shell no bigger than her smallest fingernail, some fine sand. She smiled and thought, *Amaranthus fulleris.*

As she lifted out the pile of Miss Fuller's pages, she dislodged something: One of Henry's small travelling note-books had been wedged there, between the pages. The pebbly leather had been smoothed to shiny patches where her brother's left hand had held it open as he wrote with his right. As she put her own hand where her brother's had been a moan came from somewhere, from her own throat, as if she had just that moment lost him.

On the first page were her own joking words about the train from that hot day in 1850; then the following in Henry's hand:

> *25 Jul.*
> · *Sad bcs. <u>not</u> sad*
> · *Not Tragedy. Tr. large & <u>human</u>; this <u>nature</u> & not human, tho' large*
> · *Sailors liked her, praised her, <u>loved</u> her*

- *Sailors shaved almost bald. A mourning ritual of the salty fraternity?*
- *Bolton, a sailor, has circled the world 2X. Orig. fr. Kentucky; likes Marseilles best bcs. cheap wine & wife there*
- *Study rip currents and undertow. Visible sometimes even w/out gales — gales far out can cause a rip, or an undertow? Are they same?*
- *Current running a pale green almost white w/ lavender lights, sideways, parallel to shore*
- *Candle in tide, swirl'd by waves like whelk-shell, or barber pole*
- *2 buttons fr. Ossoli's coat, jet, real but not <u>actual</u>*
- *Ellery & Arthur arrivd*

26 Jul.
- *Argument about the boy's corpse: Arthur will dig up & take coffin home tho' Ellery & I see a greater poetry in leaving it here where his parents died*
- *All frantic for book ms*

28 Jul.
- *Women cant have the Wild within*
- *Found & buried in sand a woman's arm & hand. M's? 7 Crow Brothers: The sister's finger bone whittled to open the door*
- *M told me she did have Wild — so why Europe?*

Old World not The Wild, The Wild is interior &
wards westly. M did <u>not</u> have Wild
· Sorry I never liked M
· Crab shells, bird skeletons, this stuff, not actual.
Goat when alive: Actual. Smells hwvr both alive
& dead. Not Real when Dead? The Wild can
also contain Death

The rest were his notes on weather, tides, birds, kelp, shells, grasses, the formation of dunes (with tiny drawings and arrows), and a local story about a beached whale. Nothing more about Miss Fuller.

Tenderly, she placed Henry's note-book beside the wasps' nest on the mahogany side-board where the Bratcher plate and service had once shone.

Then she sat for many minutes, with the stack of pages in her lap, still not sure whether or not to read the words of this long-dead, alarming, annoying, still-alive woman. And she went for a walk with the dog to think some more.

———

"Complete," she said aloud, and the dripping wet dog turned to look at her. "What is that?" He cocked his head at the question, or more likely at the stick she raised to throw again. She threw the stick, and turned back, now in a hurry. The dog swerved from his play and followed her.

Not pausing to take off her boots and hat, she returned to her work-room. The dog, sensing her mood as one that meant he must be quiet, found his usual place on the worn Turkey carpet next to the wood-stove and put his nose upon his paws.

She pulled the stack of pages out and began to read words formed in a large, looping hand: ". . . How extraordinary to be on board and coming home! Here I must compose my thoughts. . . . Yet still I hesitate. Not from shame, but from something else — a fear of offending, a fear of disturbing the peace of so dear a friend. . . ."

Anne read all the pages, more than forty sheets scrawled across two sides. At some point, quite unconsciously, she removed her hat and boots. She curled up in an arm-chair, the pages piled in her lap, and read that way for an hour or so; then, stiffening in that posture, returned to the chair at the table. When Mattie put her head round the door in the early afternoon she knew by the set of Anne's back not to disturb her. Anne did not eat or drink, and she felt weak and sick when she at last stopped. It was dusk. She stretched, and still in her stocking-feet stepped out on the back door-step with the collie-dog, just in time to see the last pink and orange smears over a black horizon-cloud in the west.

A little later, carrying a pot of tea and a plate of cold pork, pickles, and green beans, Anne returned to her work-room. She re-read the pages by lamp-light, while the expected storm crashed around the house, briefly. At last she went to bed.

Some days later, on a rainy morning in mid-October, a letter arrived from Anne's difficult daughter in the Wyoming territories declaring that, as women there had the vote, she was campaigning for a district council seat. She added that one day, when Wyoming became a state, she hoped to be governor. Chewing over this preposterous news, Anne bound Miss Fuller's pages up in butcher's paper and tied them with strong twine. On the top she wrote: **PRIVATE PAPERS OF MARGARET FULLER OSSOLI**.

She had heard of an organization recently founded, The New England Society for the Progress of Women. With her other daughter — the clever, handsome one — she braved the rain that afternoon, to attend a tea at the Society's modest house in Cambridge, and while the speaker droned about conditions in the New South, she slipped into the library-office of the director. She took the bundle from her carpet-bag and placed it in a low cupboard, on a shelf underneath other papers. It did not look as though these shelves were dusted often, but one never knew. Evening was coming on already, and the rain blew against the window of the office. She shivered.

As soon as next month, perhaps, the Society might move to a new building, or rearrange its offices, and the ladies would sort and pack these shelves. Someone would find the bundle and send it to a local scholar, a historian. Possibly that historian would be interested; possibly he would read it. Possibly he would give it to a woman of his acquaintance, herself educated and a believer in the rights of women, and she would know what to do with it.

Or perhaps one day the Society's maids would be told to clear out all those old papers. One of the maids, educated even if only slightly, would notice the label and call the bundle to the attention of the house-keeper, who would authoritatively drop it in the dustbin.

Or the Society's house would go up in flames on some cold night five years hence.

Or the shelves would never be sorted, and the Society's building would return to private hands. It would be home to a large and boisterous family. One wintry day, the children would need extra paper for snow-flakes and paper dolls, and would cut page after page into delicate shreds.

———

Miss Fuller did not inhabit Anne's night-time dreams. (Those were populated almost exclusively by members of her family and by a boy she had loved when she was fifteen, a glorious laughing boy visiting relatives in Concord, who had climbed into a pear-tree and thrown fruit at her and then pulled her under a wagon to kiss her.) But once she was fully awake, her first thought was often of that woman.

It was Anne's morning habit to make a pot of tea and take it into her work-room. She drew the curtains back on the clear north light, tied her duster into place, and set up the paints — daubing oil into cyan blue and Indian yellow powders, shaving off curls of Japanese lacquer for the red tints, thinning out the white with pine spirits, to make the misty white-into-grey gruel of sea foam.

If you could have visited, you would have seen the stacks of worked and half-worked canvases, dried and set aside, and if you had leafed through them — but can one be said to leaf through those heavy things, so much heavier than leaves? — you would have seen how her theme had seized her. For again and again, as long as she was able to paint, in the years until rheumatism froze her fingers, she worked on the same image.

We are in a shallow but wild sea. The vantage point of the viewer is slightly behind and to one side of the central figure, a woman — so it is as if the viewer, standing in deeper water, is following her lead. The woman is partly bent and stepping through ocean waves; sometimes with her entire face visible, turned to us with a beckoning expression; in some versions one can make out the images of figures on the beach (that one looks like Henry in his old suit!); sometimes with the beach bare; sometimes with a bell-buoy or a life-boat visible; sometimes with the light of a sunrise rouging the tips of the waves, but always:

A woman, her hair streaming in the wind and water, her

red dress half torn away and soaked nearly to black, clasping a book under one bare arm and a small child in the other — a woman, thus encumbered, yet striding through the boiling waves, and making it to shore.

AUTHOR'S NOTE

Though grounded in fact, this is a work of fiction. To readers interested in history I recommend Margaret Fuller's writings and the biographies of her written by Charles Capper and by Paula Blanchard; Alexander Herzen's memoirs; Megan Marshall's biography of the Peabody sisters; Brenda Wineapple's biography of Hawthorne; and the biographical and critical writings on Thoreau and Emerson by Stanley Cavell, Walter Harding, Jonathan Levin, Joel Porte, and many other scholars.

I wish to thank: Patricia Willis at the Beinecke Library at Yale University, Pamela Matz at the Widener Library at Harvard University, and the librarians at the Houghton Library at Harvard, for invaluable assistance; and The Corporation of Yaddo and The MacDowell Colony, for time and peace in which to work.

Many thanks to my agent, Jin Auh, and to the wonderful Steerforth Press team of Roland Pease and Chip Fleischer.

Douglas Bauer, Christopher Benfey, Catherine Ciepiela, Annabel Davis-Goff, Richard Q. Ford, Lyndall Gordon, Elana Greenfield, Alice Mattison, Marc Robinson, Elizabeth Sacre, and Mark Wunderlich provided help of various and essential kinds, and I am profoundly grateful.

It was Joel Porte's inspired writing and teaching that "shocked my soul awake" to the lives and work of nineteenth-century American writers when I was an undergraduate; to him I owe my longest-standing debt and offer my deepest thanks.

All errors and fancies are my own.

OTHER BOOKS BY APRIL BERNARD

Fiction
Pirate Jenny

Poetry
Blackbird Bye Bye
Psalms
Swan Electric
Romanticism

A NOTE ABOUT THE AUTHOR

April Bernard is a novelist, poet, and essayist. Her first novel, *Pirate Jenny*, was published in 1990 and her poetry collections include *Romanticism*, *Blackbird Bye Bye*, *Psalms*, and *Swan Electric*. Her work has appeared in numerous journals, including *The New York Review of Books*, *The New Yorker*, *The New York Times*, *The New Republic*, *The Nation*, and *Slate*. Her honors include a Guggenheim award, the Walt Whitman Award from the Academy of American Poets, a Whitney Humanities Fellowship at Yale University, a Sidney Harman Fellowship, and the Stover Prize. She is Director of Creative Writing at Skidmore College and is on the faculty of the Bennington MFA Writing Seminars.